The
EDGE
of the
SILVER
SEA

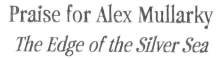

Praise for Alex Mullarky
The Edge of the Silver Sea

"Sparkling with myth, magic and the wonder of wild places, this enchanting tale will make readers look at the world with glittering eyes."

– Sophie Anderson, Carnegie-shortlisted author of *The House with Chicken Legs*

"A clever twist on Scottish folklore... If you like faery bargains, fantastic creatures and wild magic, you will love this book!"

– Skye McKenna, author of *Hedgewitch*

 ## *The Sky Beneath the Stone*

"*The Sky Beneath the Stone* is beautiful, bright and brilliant – a perfect blend of magic, adventure and heart, with a gorgeous Cumbrian setting, a wonderful weaving of nature, folklore and history, heart-lifting incidental inclusivity, and OS grid references at the start of each chapter so you can map the journey! It is one of those books I want to press into every young reader's hands, because I know so many of them will fall in love with it."

– Sophie Anderson, Carnegie-shortlisted author of *The House with Chicken Legs*

*For my parents, who brought me to the magic,
and in memory of Rouk, the best bad kelpie.*

Kelpies is an imprint of Floris Books
First published in 2024 by Floris Books
© 2024 Alex Mullarky
Author photo courtesy of Alex Mullarky
Map © 2024 Floris Books
Alex Mullarky has asserted their right under the
Copyright, Designs and Patent Act 1988 to be
identified as the Author of this Work

 Also available as an eBook

British Library CIP data available
ISBN 978-178250-917-2
Printed in Poland through Hussar

Printed on sustainably
sourced FSC® certified
paper. Uses plant-based
inks which reduce
chemical emissions.

MIX
Paper from
responsible sources
FSC® C167221
FSC
www.fsc.org

The
EDGE
of the
SILVER
SEA

ALEX MULLARKY

Kelpies

WHALEBONE
BAY

Selkies

Kelpie

LOCH

THE VILLAGE
OF ROSCOE

RIVER IRVING

Cù-Sìth
(Coo-Shee)

ALASDAIR'S
HOUSE

SHOP

HARBOUR

N
W   E
S

Cat-Sìth
(Cat-Shee)

Bean Nighe
(Ben Nee-Yeh)

SEA LOCH

Fiadh Mho'r
(Fee-ugh Vore)

THE CREACHANNS

LOCH

LOCH

Irving

STANDING
STONE

Will-o'-the-wisps

Cailleach
(Kal-Yuch)

...OCH GUEST HOUSE

...HE SEA STAG INN

THE
STEADING

Crodh Mara
(Cro Mara)

TO THE →
MAINLAND

THE ISLE of
ROSCOE

THE LEGENDARY ISLE

The legendary isle of Roscoe was cloaked in mist. Blair Zielinski stood at the prow of the ferry, gripping the cold metal railing. Every passing second brought her closer to the place her parents had been talking about all her life, but she couldn't see a thing.

In the poster that had always hung above their mantelpiece, Roscoe's vivid emerald and lavender hills rose from a silver sea. Before Blair now, white-capped waves rolled over the steel-grey Atlantic, blurring into a dark sky streaked with rain. She squinted into the cloud, waiting for the island to reveal itself.

The ferry lurched as another huge wave rolled under it, and Blair clung tight to the railing. She'd been too nauseous to stay inside the cabin as the boat swayed, but she wasn't sure she was any better off out here, with rain driving into her face and soaking her clothes.

When Blair looked up again, shapes were starting to appear through the cloud. The hills of Roscoe loomed over her, much closer than she'd expected, and suddenly they were silhouetted by a bright burst of lightning.

Just for a moment, Blair thought she saw something on the ridge of the highest hill – a stag with great antlers, or the tall figure of a human, or something between the two. The hairs on the back of Blair's neck rose as she peered up at the hillside and felt a strange certainty that the figure peered back.

But it was only a brief flash, and then the hills were murky shapes once more. Blair tried to shake off the uneasy feeling that she was being watched.

A low rumble of thunder grew until it felt like it was vibrating through her very bones, sending her heart skittering. She had to admit defeat. It was no use scaring herself out here, where she might be pitched overboard at any moment.

Blair retreated to the cabin, her glasses steaming up as she stepped inside. The few passengers were all getting to their feet. It was time to return to their cars.

As the ferry ramp lowered with a shriek, Blair sat in the passenger seat of the rented moving van beside her dad. She had an uncomfortable suspicion that anyone could guess they were related: it was their messy, mousy hair, their fair skin and rounded faces, and a slight hunch in the way they sat.

Discarded on the middle seat was a folded timetable for the ferry. While her dad navigated the rickety ramp onto the harbour, Blair slipped it into the pocket of her damp denim jacket. Her dad glanced over and she pretended to be adjusting one of her badges – the one that read OUR PLANET! OUR FUTURE! SCHOOL STRIKE FOR CLIMATE.

"Here we go," her dad said as they hit the cobbles. "After all these years!"

The worst of the storm seemed to have passed: the thunder had moved away, but the world was still mired in drizzle as they followed a small yellow hatchback, piloted by Blair's mum, into the village of Roscoe.

The village had the same name as the island because it was the only village *on* the island and, from what Blair had gathered, the only really habitable part of it. There was just one road, overgrown lanes branching off it leading to long, low houses with lumpy, whitewashed walls and windows in their sloping roofs. At the edge of the harbour were the island's only shop and a pub. There were a few bed and breakfasts in a row, but Blair observed no signs of life other than a calico cat sitting on a fence post, watching them pass.

This place was a ghost town. Did it really need *another* B&B?

Worse still, the hatchback and the van continued past the village. The road became a winding, single-track lane leading seemingly to nowhere, bordered by a restless sea on one side and bleak moorland on the other.

Blair dug her phone out of her pocket and angled the screen away from her dad.

She had a message from Libby. It was a video of her best friend rehearsing a silly dance routine, and there was a message underneath.

> gonna dance outside the bank dressed as a polar bear! they're still investing in fossil fuels

Blair quickly tapped out a response.

> losers. wish I was there :'(

A red exclamation mark lit up her screen. No signal.

"There it is!" Blair's dad cried in excitement. He gave her knee a squeeze, which startled her into looking up.

The van was slowing, which made sense as the road appeared to be ending. As a matter of fact, Blair couldn't think of a time she had seen the *end* of a road before. The tarmac disappeared into turf, which rolled under a stone wall inset with an iron gate. Beyond that stood the house that Blair's parents had bought without their daughter ever having seen it.

Blair was surprised to discover that there was another level her heart could sink to. The sprawling, dilapidated farmhouse looked like it had had rooms added on at random over the course of a very long life. The exterior was dull and grey, the garden wild and overgrown.

Piles of junk spilled from the outbuildings onto the grass in the front.

It seemed like no one had lived here for a long, long time. Blair's parents had never mentioned that.

"It's a fixer-upper, all right," said her dad delightedly. "I remember when we first laid eyes on this house thirteen years ago, Blair. On our holiday not long after you were born. I thought, *Now that place has potential.*"

The hatchback parked up in front of them. By the time Blair had climbed out of the van, her mum was already gazing up at the house, hands on hips. The frown lines around her eyes seemed fainter than usual as she said, "It's bigger than I remembered."

Blair pulled her jacket tighter against the wind, but her parents didn't even seem to notice the miserable weather.

"See how much has been done already, myszka." Blair's dad gestured to a fresh patch of black tiles on the roof. "That was all collapsed – uninhabitable!"

"It's a miracle it's ready for us to move in," her mum remarked.

Her dad nodded gravely. "It certainly is, when every builder in the Hebrides is convinced our house is cursed."

"Cursed?" Blair repeated. They'd never mentioned *that* either.

Her mum waved them onwards, ignoring Blair. "Let's get inside."

Blair trailed her parents up the overgrown garden path. Her dad unlocked the front door and turned to Blair, gesturing her through first.

Blair stepped through the porch into the shadowy kitchen. Wires dangled from the ceiling, which was stained brown in patches. Beside the old stove, tiles were cracked and missing from the wall. Cupboard doors hung from their hinges, and the lino flooring was burnt and peeling. Her dad was looking to her for a reaction, but she couldn't find any words.

Her mum bustled in behind them and moved determinedly to the window above the sink. "All it needs is a little light," she said, pushing back the curtains, then cutting short a shriek as a fat brown spider dropped out of the frilly pink fabric.

Her dad took a few strides deeper into the room, throwing his arms wide. "Home, sweet home!" he declared. One of his boots crunched on a snail; Blair covered her mouth and tried not to gag.

Even though it was mostly empty, there was something about the place that gave it the air of being freshly abandoned. A painting of deer on a hillside still hung crookedly from a hook, and a single shoe waited beside the porch. Blair felt like an intruder.

Her parents gave her a tour of their plans for the B&B, but most of it went in one ear and out the other as Blair turned her unresponsive phone over in her hands. Through the hallway were the pantry, a bathroom, and two rooms destined to become a sitting room and the breakfast room. Upstairs, three guest rooms, another bathroom and her parents' bedroom. In the attic, up a narrow staircase, they planned to install *another* two bedrooms.

There would be a lot of strangers around, basically. "Where do I sleep?" Blair asked, suddenly troubled by the realisation that they hadn't pointed out a space for her.

With conspiratory smiles, her parents led her back down to the ground floor, into the kitchen. At the far side was a door Blair hadn't noticed. Her mum pushed it open, beckoning for Blair to take a closer look.

She stared through the doorway at a bare room with a window looking out to sea, and no furniture besides an ancient, lopsided wardrobe against one wall.

"Your own wing!" her dad said from behind her.

"A bit more private here, isn't it?" her mum added. "Out of the way."

Out of your *way*, Blair thought.

"What do you think?" her dad prodded.

Blair shrugged. "Yeah."

Her dad's laugh was incredulous. "Yeah?!"

Blair's mum cleared her throat. "If we could have brought you with us to view the place you know we would have. But we knew this was the house of our dreams and we had to make a quick decision—"

"It's fine," Blair cut over her. Hearing her mum trying to be reasonable was almost too much to bear. She did what she had to do: she bared her teeth in what she hoped was a convincing smile. Then she reached for the handle and gently closed the door in her parents' hopeful faces. A moment later she heard them shuffling away and their voices raised in exclamation over something new.

Blair turned back to the room and took a deep breath.

The rain had picked up again and was lashing against the window, the wind howling beyond.

She pulled her phone out of her pocket. No messages, no notifications – no signal.

She was hundreds of miles from the only home she'd ever known, and she couldn't even send a message to the friends she'd had to leave behind.

She couldn't help it. Hot tears were rolling down her face before she could stop them. Blair pushed her glasses up her head and dashed the tears away with the back of one hand.

Cheep!

Blair froze. The sound was loud and sharp and animal.

Were there birds nesting in the rafters? She glanced through the window but couldn't see anything nest-like. And it had sounded so close…

Cheep!

She jerked around – she hadn't imagined the sound. Could it have been a mouse? But she hadn't seen anything move.

Cheep!

There it was again! The sound, more urgent than before, echoed like it was in a chamber.

Blair's eyes landed on the tilting wardrobe against the far wall. She approached it warily, laid her hand on the doorknob and then pulled it open in one quick movement, ready to confront whatever lay in wait inside.

Light from the room flooded into the dark cupboard and revealed only a single furry, moth-eaten coat hanging at one end of the rail. The back of the cupboard was missing, and there was a crack in the stone where light shone through from the world beyond.

The gap in the wall was filled with dried grass and moss, sculpted into a cosy round space.

A nest.

Cheep!

Blair looked down and there, on the base of the wardrobe, was a little pink alien: a baby bird, fresh as anything, only a little feather fluff on its jellyfish body. She wondered if that meant it was freshly hatched.

"Hello there," said Blair. The bird wriggled and chirped at her again. She peeked into the nest and saw fragments of pale eggshell; her suspicions were confirmed. But if it was that fresh, it must have fallen out of the nest, and there was no way it was going to get back up.

Blair crouched down. She was surprised by the way her heart sped up when she reached for the creature, by the hesitation she felt before she scooped the soft, warm body into her palms. She paused for a moment, feeling the little life in her hands. The bird was quiet; its eyes were closed, and it seemed soothed by her touch, calmly radiating heat like a tiny hot water bottle. But then its eyes opened, and her breath caught. They were pale violet, shockingly bright, like heather shot through with an electric current. She hadn't known there were birds with eyes like that.

Blair cleared a patch of eggshell so that she could deposit the little creature gently into the centre of the nest. "There you go," she said as she set it down. There was no sign of another chick or any other eggs. She wondered whether she ought to get some food and water for it. But what would it eat? She had no idea what kind of bird it was. Besides which, it was bound to have parents.

Where were they, though?

"Out finding food, probably," she reasoned to herself under her breath.

The safest thing to do was wait, and hopefully they would return to take care of it soon.

"Try not to fall out of your nest again, okay?" she told it.

The bird stared at her with those strange eyes, but it didn't make another sound.

Gently, Blair closed the wardrobe.

ROSCOE NEEDS YOU

Blair slept in until late the next morning and then couldn't quite muster the will to get up. Instead she constantly refreshed the secret email account and messaging app she and her friends used for protest planning, but nothing would load. Eventually she rolled out from under the covers of her newly assembled bed and began to unpack her art supplies: notebooks and sketchpads, scrap paper and cardboard, glue and spray cans and markers, pastels, brushes and chalks.

It was a long time before she realised, with a flash of shame, that she'd forgotten to check on her new roommate. But when she threw open the scratched wooden doors, the baby bird was sitting comfortably in its nest. It looked a bit darker now, the beginnings of blue feathers on its little pink body. It cheeped happily when it saw her, but there was still no sign of its mother.

"Sorry I'm late, little dude," Blair muttered. The little creature seemed just as bright and energetic as it had yesterday. If it wasn't being fed, surely it would be looking tired and weak by now. The parents were just being sneaky, clearly. They must spend their days hunting – that explained why Blair wasn't seeing them.

"I would leave this open so we could keep each other company, but I don't want to scare your parents away," Blair told the bird. "I'm right on the other side of these doors, all right? If you get into any trouble, you just let me know."

The bird chirped again – she could have sworn it was agreeing. Blair rolled her eyes at herself and shut the doors.

With her phone basically useless she was going to need something else to distract her. The cardboard box from her new bed was resting against the wall, just crying out to be turned into something beautiful. Blair grabbed it, along with a few tubes of paint, and braced herself for the outside world. Her parents weren't around when she opened her bedroom door, but she thought she could hear them moving about upstairs as she walked down the hallway and let herself into the back garden.

At least it wasn't raining any more. There were two trees behind the house, neither of them as tall as the roof yet, with thin trunks and cracked silver bark. They looked ghostly in the overgrown tangle that was their new garden. Blair heard waves beating against the shore, and the drawn-out cry of a seabird.

Back home in Carlisle, when she'd stepped into her garden she'd heard music and chatter, the sounds of a hundred lives being lived all around her. The quiet here was desolate and strange.

Focusing on her work, Blair tore the long cardboard box in half and set it out on the ground like a canvas. She tore off another small piece, squeezed some cobalt blue paint onto it, and dipped in her brush.

Nothing made her feel steadier than preparing for a protest, and their rocky crossing on the ferry the day before had given her an idea for a banner. Lettering was Blair's thing: slanting paint strokes, bold colours.

THE OCEANS ARE RISING AND SO ARE WE!

"Oh Blair, what is this?"

A voice from the doorway. Blair glanced back and saw her mum frowning at her.

"Just practice, Mum."

Her mum walked over and picked up the sign. Her face creased. When she spoke, her voice was heavy with frustration. "We give you a day to settle in, don't even ask for your help when we have a whole house to turn around, and you decide to spend it on this? Have you even looked around, Blair? Do you realise how lucky you are to be here?"

"Lucky?!" Blair repeated. "I have no signal, no internet, I can't even speak to anyone! How am I supposed to do anything from here?"

"You're in one of the most remote, wild places in the whole country! Isn't this the exact thing you and your friends are fighting for? I thought you'd like… that you'd—" Her mum's voice broke and she stopped speaking, shaking her head in silence.

Blair grabbed the sign from her mum and stormed back into the house, where she folded it up and shoved it angrily into the bin.

"There's no need to make a scene!" her mum said, following her in. Her dad appeared at the foot of the stairs, looking uncertainly between the two of them.

Blair opened her mouth to retort, but there was a brisk knock at the front door.

Her mum leapt forward to answer it. "Are we expecting anyone?"

She opened the front door to reveal a stout woman with fawn skin seated in a wheelchair. She had a neat grey bob beneath a flat cap, and wore a lavender cardigan with a long floral skirt and short, green wellington boots.

"Morag Duncan," she said. "Pleased to meet you." She held out her hand and Blair's mum shook it.

"Anna Zielinski," she replied. Blair was always startled to be reminded that her mum had a name that was not, in fact, Mum.

Morag was already peering around her into the kitchen; Blair's dad crossed the room to greet her with one hand outstretched.

"Józef Zielinski. It's a pleasure to meet you. Would you like to come in?"

Morag propelled her wheelchair forwards and rolled into the house, which she immediately began scanning from floor to ceiling.

"This is our daughter, Blair," her mum introduced her.

Morag nodded a greeting, though she seemed more interested in the state of the lino floor. "Shall we have a cup of tea, perhaps?"

She was already pulling herself up beside the old wooden table, and Blair's dad sat down politely opposite her. Blair's mum hovered, searching boxes for clean mugs.

"I wanted to introduce myself, as your nearest neighbour," said Morag. "Although you are a way out on your own here, aren't you!" she chuckled. "But it is lovely to see life being breathed into the old steading after so many years. I suppose you must be those technological types that can work from home?"

Blair's dad glanced at her mum before answering. "Actually, we're going to turn the place into a bed and breakfast," he said.

Morag sat up a little straighter. "Is that so! Well, the committee will have to be informed, of course… But you wouldn't know about the committee yet…"

"What's the committee?" Blair's mum asked. It was the first thing she had said, aside from her name, and Blair was reminded just how broad her mum's Cumbrian accent was – even more so than her own.

Her dad was not-so-subtly attempting to beckon Blair to sit down at the table, so she thunked down into the seat beside him.

"We are rather a close-knit community here on Roscoe and we like to make sure our businesses all conform to certain standards," Morag was saying. "A decade ago you wouldn't have believed the state of the village... falling to pieces! You wouldn't have recognised it, I tell you. So we formed 'Roscoe Needs You', our little group, to get the place up to scratch." She scrutinised the room again, and it was clear from the crook of one eyebrow that she was finding it wanting.

"We'll have to review your plans, make sure there are no conflicts of interest, and then an inspection before you open for business. I suppose you'll be wanting to do that as soon as possible, what with the festival on the way."

"Of course, the Wild Roscoe Festival!" Blair's dad nodded. "That's right. We're aiming to tidy the place up over the summer and take in our first guests a few days before the festival begins." Somehow, despite being raised by a Polish father and a Scottish mother in the north of England, Blair's dad managed to speak without any noticeable accent at all.

"Oh, essential, absolutely essential," Morag agreed. "Wildlife watchers come from far and wide for festival month – it's the busiest time of the year."

Blair ran her fingers along the table's apron, which was full of divots and marks. Her fingers caught on a deep scratch and she tilted her head to get a better look at it. Someone had carved the initials *A.R.* a long time ago.

"Well, we'll make an effort to open our doors as early as possible," her mum said as she began pouring the tea.

"Do you take sugar?"

"Two teaspoons, please," Morag said. "Yes, I should certainly advise it." She nodded her thanks as Blair's mum passed her a steaming mug. "I run a modest guest house on the edge of the village, as a matter of fact. We're often overbooked, and this is just the kind of quaint little place – once it's all done up, of course – that I might recommend to my surplus guests. Come and pay me a visit when you've the time. I'd be happy to show you around and give you some advice."

"That's very kind!" said Blair's mum.

Morag sipped her tea, winced, and then cast her eyes around the room again. Blair felt the moment their neighbour's gaze landed on her.

"And how old are you, Blair?" Morag asked.

"Thirteen," Blair answered. Her mum pushed a mug of tea across to her, and Blair topped it up generously with oat milk and sugar.

"Thirteen! My, my… Must be more than a decade since my youngest was your age. I remember how bored she used to get in the summer holidays, so I had her help me with the guest house every day. Your parents must be very grateful to have you."

Blair smiled as she lifted her mug to her lips, leaving it to her parents to field that one.

"It's an adjustment for all of us," her dad said diplomatically. "From the city out to an island as remote as this one… You can imagine!"

"I truly cannot," Morag said primly, taking another

tentative sip. "I've only been to the mainland a handful of times. Roscoe has always been my home."

Blair kept the mug in front of her face, hiding her mouth as her smile faded away. She tried to envision a future in which she was tethered to this island for the rest of her life; it made her stomach drop.

She stood up abruptly. "I've got to finish sorting my room out."

"*Now*, Blair?" her mum said in disbelief.

"Sorry," Blair said, making a swift exit.

She needed to get out of this house.

ARTIST OR ECOLOGIST

Blair's escape was much easier than she'd expected, and slightly anticlimactic. She pushed her bedroom window open as wide as it would go, threw a leg over the windowsill and pulled herself out. With a grumbled mixture of dismay and relief, she fought her way through the brambles and hopped over the garden wall.

She shifted the backpack on her shoulders as she surveyed the open landscape that stretched ahead of her. Beyond their garden there were no walls, no fences. The undulating land hid the distant village from sight; theirs could have been the only house in the world. The moor rolled away from her, sloping up into a low rocky hill.

The strange figure she'd seen on the hilltop during the storm flashed briefly in her mind, but she banished the thought. Surely she'd be able to get some signal up there.

Blair kept her head down as she walked. It didn't take long to realise she was not equipped for Roscoe weather. The wind whipped her hair across her face and cut straight through her denim jacket. She jumped as her trainers squelched into a patch of bog and her toes went cold. Charting a new course around the shiny silver puddles and clumps of reeds, she folded her arms tightly across her chest.

Out of breath and near the top of the hill, Blair looked back the way she'd come. From here there was a good view of the bay and the house, and the village was in sight in the distance. A tall, rectangular stone at the summit helpfully offered shelter from the wind, so she sat down beside it and pulled out her phone.

No service.

Blair swallowed, shoving the phone back into her pocket. Libby would know what to do. Everything would be easier if she could just hear her voice.

There must at least be signal in the village; she'd have to get back there, one way or another. But since she'd climbed all the way here, she may as well make the most of it. She had a sketchbook and some markers in her backpack; she could draw until she calmed down.

As Blair took in the view and began to translate its shapes to paper, it occurred to her just how quiet it was here, out of the wind, away from the beating of the waves on the shore. It was eerie, the way her pen scratched noisily across the paper.

There was a sound like bored kids pulling up grass on the playing fields. Blair looked up, and a flicker of movement made her eyes shift focus.

Deer! And they were right in front of her, just slightly further down the hillside. There were two of them, and somehow they were so much bigger than she'd ever imagined. Her heart picked up speed. They were grazing on the peaty turf, blending in with their burnished red fur.

Holding her breath, Blair turned to a fresh page in her sketchbook and quickly began to outline the shapes of their bodies. But she was disturbed by another sound that rang out in the silence.

Chuck-chuck.

Like a startled hare, she scanned the landscape around her.

There, half-hidden behind some rocks, light bounced off a camera lens. Behind the camera and mostly obscured by it was a boy, about her own age. As she watched, he paused and waved at her.

Hesitantly, Blair waved back. But even though he'd put down his camera, there was a flash in the air between them. A twinkling light that flickered for a long moment and then went out. Blair blinked hard, unsure what she had just seen.

The boy said something, but it was too quiet for Blair to hear. She shook her head.

"Will-o'-the-wisp," he said, louder.

The deer bolted.

Blair felt a bite of disappointment as the deer vanished around the hill. "What did you say?"

The boy walked over to her. She was probably right that he was about her age, though he was a bit shorter, with pale skin and a mop of sandy hair. He wore khaki combat trousers and a loose fleece jacket with a hole where a pocket should be, zipped right up to his chin.

"That light. Folk call them will-o'-the-wisps. Supposedly they'll lead you safely through the bog," he said. He was softly spoken, and the lilt of his voice was different to the Scottish accents she had heard before.

"Will they?" Blair replied.

The boy scoffed. "Not likely. It's a trick of the light – phosphorescence caused by gas escaping from the peat."

Blair wasn't quite sure what to say to that. "Right."

He grinned. "I'm Alasdair. Alasdair Reid. I like your pin."

Blair touched the enamel rainbow flag he was pointing to. "Thanks. I'm Blair."

"Which B&B are you staying at?" he asked. "I live at the boat house, opposite the general store. It's quite early for tourists."

"I'm not a tourist." *If only.* "My family just moved here."

"Really?" His face lit up. "What year are you in?"

"Going into year nine. Um… S2, I think?"

"That's the same year as me! We'll be travelling to school together, then. It's on the next island. I bet you've never taken a ferry to school before."

He seemed to suddenly notice her sketchbook and leaned forward to peer at it. Blair closed it hastily, shoving it back into her rucksack, and stood up.

"Artist or ecologist?" he asked.

Between the unexpected question and his accent, Blair

was lost. "Sorry?"

"Species illustration?" Alasdair suggested, gesturing to her backpack. "Did you know the Roscoe red deer is its own subspecies? They're unique. Every summer the Roscoe Biodiversity Trust organises a survey of the deer to keep track of the population. It's mostly me, actually – we don't have a lot of volunteers. And I take photos for my records." He gestured to the camera.

"Oh! Well, I'm not an ecologist. I guess I am an artist, sort of. I like to make art for protests and things. I'm an activist."

"Oh." His eyebrows lifted, like he hadn't considered there could possibly be a *third* option. "You mean like the school strike stuff?"

"Yeah, exactly. Me and my friend Libby, we organised the first school strike in the north of England. We were on the news and everything."

Alasdair just started fiddling with his camera.

"Is there a group at your school?" Blair pushed.

"Um, no," Alasdair said. "If I missed school, there'd be, like, no one in my class. Besides, I don't think anyone would care if a bunch of island kids decided to protest."

"Of course they would!" Blair countered. "It's about making a statement. Showing the adults that we can't just carry on like nothing's happening."

Alasdair didn't look at her when he replied. "I don't think causing trouble for teachers is going to save the world. Besides, Roscoe's doing fine."

"You're joking, right? This is an island! We're in the

middle of the sea! Haven't you heard about melting glaciers? Habitat loss? Ocean acidification?"

"I'm not an idiot – I do actually listen in geography," Alasdair snapped.

Blair held up her hands. "Okay, it's just... Roscoe may *seem* fine for now, but you can't act like nothing's happening in the rest of the world!"

"Typical," Alasdair muttered.

"What's typical?"

Alasdair finally met her eyes. "Incomers moving in and telling us how we should be doing things. How long have you been here, a day?"

Only just, but Blair wasn't about to tell him that. "I'm not the one pretending to care about nature and then looking down on people who are actually taking action!"

"Holding up a sign doesn't achieve anything."

"Well, taking photos of deer isn't going to protect them from climate disaster!"

Blair's fists clenched as they faced off against each other. Alasdair drew in a breath, but before he could make her any angrier, Blair spun on her heel and stormed away.

It wasn't long before the boy was out of sight behind the rocks. Blair's breaths were coming fast, and not just from her stumbling steps over the uneven terrain. Desperate to hear a friendly voice, she pulled her phone out of her pocket. She still had no data, but there was a single bar of signal. She'd have to do this the old-fashioned way.

She scrolled down to Libby's number and hit dial.

There was a long silence as she held the phone to her ear. Finally, when she was just about to give up completely, it started to ring. Blair held a clenched fist to her chest. *Pick up.*

"Blair! Are you actually phoning me?"

"There's no data out here, Libby! I'm literally calling you from the top of a mountain."

"That's tragic. How will you survive?"

"Don't joke! As if you wouldn't struggle too."

"All right, I know. Look, we've been talking in the group chat—"

"You heard the part about *no data*, right?"

"Don't you have WiFi?"

"No! Mum and Tata say it won't be installed until the end of summer. The phone engineer only comes out from the mainland every couple of months. I couldn't believe it."

"Well, you are in the middle of the Atlantic Ocean. Anyway, we were messaging today. The next strike is going to be BIG. Get this: we're going to skip the first day of school!"

Blair sighed heavily. "That's such a cool idea."

"We're gonna be working on it all summer. We're going to screen-print flags and T-shirts, make banners, and Theresa had an idea for giant animal skeleton puppets that we can carry with us on the march. It's going to be the biggest one yet! We're having a meeting about it the day after tomorrow."

Libby's voice had started to break up a bit, so Blair hovered in place, terrified of losing her only bar. "But I want to help," she said, knowing she sounded awkwardly desperate. "If I can just be at the meeting to plan with you guys, maybe there are things I can make while I'm out here. Do you think I could stay with you?"

The line went silent for a moment and Blair worried she'd lost her, but then Libby spoke again. "I dunno, Blair. Do you think your parents would let you come back so soon? Isn't it, like, really expensive to get the ferry and the train and everything?"

Blair swallowed, ignoring all the obvious red flags that were already popping up in her mind. "Let me figure that out. Will your parents mind if I stay with you?"

Her phone beeped twice in answer. Whatever Libby might have been about to say was lost. No signal.

SEAWEED

By the time Blair got back to the house it was evening, but the sky was just as bright as it had been all day. Her parents had warned her the Scottish summers would be like this, but it was still jarring.

Beside the house was a long, low building that had once been a stable or something like that. The heavy doors had been forced open, and she could hear her parents rummaging around within. In the version of the story she'd let Libby believe, this was where she'd ask them for permission to make a trip back to the mainland.

But she wasn't going to do that, because she already knew what their answer would be. Which really only left her with one option.

Blair slipped into the house and closed the door gently behind her. She crept up the stairs and let herself into her parents' darkened bedroom, where their belongings were still stacked up in boxes.

She was fairly certain where she would find what she

was looking for. She'd stumbled across it many times before while digging through her parents' clothes, looking for things to wear – their stuff was old enough to be retro, and very comfy. Plus, everyone knew that second-hand fashion was the most sustainable.

Blair searched until she found a box marked **SOCKS**, then peeled the parcel tape carefully from the cardboard and opened it up. She dug around until her fingers brushed something cold and solid.

It was an old jam jar, cleaned out long ago, with a peeling white label that read *Blair's University Fund*. The jar was stuffed with twenty pound notes – not a neat wad of cash, but squashed together as though each note had been pushed in with the others once it had been earned.

Blair stared at it uncertainly, for a moment forgetting why she was doing this. But then she remembered the expression on her mum's face when she'd held Blair's sign in her hands: so far from proud, or impressed… Just unhappy. Blair clenched her teeth and twisted the lid off the jar. This money was for her future, after all, and her future was the *exact* reason she had to be at this meeting. She dug out a small handful of notes, stuffing them straight into her pocket.

"Blair?" her dad's voice echoed from the garden. Her cheeks heating, she twisted the lid back on and shoved the jar deep into the box, then raced downstairs.

Blair met her dad just as he reached the front door. "Come and look at this," he said warmly, guiding her outside.

Junk was scattered across the grass outside the open doors to the outbuildings, from antique farm tools to stacks of plastic plant pots. Blair's mum stood out the front, propping up a Blair-sized bicycle with a thin blue frame and a rusted metal basket. She rang the bell – it was heavily rusted too, more of a croak than a ring.

"Look what we found for you!" Her dad threw his arms out towards the bike. "Perfect for you to get in and out of the village!"

Surprised, Blair smiled weakly. She could feel the stolen notes rustling in her pocket.

"Try it out!" her dad insisted.

Blair obediently climbed onto the bike, set her feet to the pedals and rode it down the garden path. Somehow, the tyres weren't flat. She stopped by the gate and looked out at the winding road towards the village. It probably wouldn't take her more than ten minutes with a set of wheels.

"Sustainable travel. How about that?" her dad said.

"She needs a helmet," her mum added.

Blair's smile grew broader, even though her mum was talking about her like she wasn't there.

"This is *exactly* what I need," she said.

The sea was still when Blair looked out of her window early the following morning, and mist hung low over the water.

She opened the wardrobe doors and the baby bird chirped a greeting. It no longer looked quite as fresh –

today it was a ball of blue-grey fluff. There was still no sign that it was struggling to survive: its eyes were bright and its body plump as it wriggled around in its mossy nest.

"You are a mystery," Blair murmured. "I wish my parents would give me as much space as yours."

She glanced over at the packed rucksack waiting by her bedroom door and sucked in her bottom lip. The bird's violet eyes locked on hers the moment she turned back. It chirped sadly.

"Don't make this hard!" Blair pleaded. "You're going to be fine. You're a fighter, and I am too. But I can't fight from here. I'll only be gone a few days – you just need to stay safe until then, all right?"

The bird had nothing to say; it wriggled around in its nest until it was facing away from her. Blair tried not to take that personally. She didn't appreciate the wrench in her chest as she closed the wardrobe doors.

When Blair stepped out into the morning the grass around her trainers was glittering with dew, and she could just about glimpse a pocket of blue sky through the mist.

She tapped her pocket to make sure the ferry timetable was still in place, took the old bike from where it was leaning up against the wall of the house and wheeled it down the garden path. The gate squeaked as she closed it behind her.

Blair flinched, casting a worried glance at her parents' bedroom window. When the curtains didn't flicker, she hopped onto the bike and pedalled furiously down the road, not looking back.

Once she was moving the anxiety left her, and she sucked in the crisp air. She could feel sunshine on her cheeks; the fog was burning away already. The morning was beautiful. Everything seemed to have a rosy glow now that she was heading home.

The road to the village was longer than Blair remembered. She'd felt like she'd been cycling for a while already, but lingering mist still cloaked the path ahead, and there was no sign of the cluster of limewashed buildings.

Blair slammed on the brakes, checked her watch and pulled out the ferry timetable, wondering how many minutes she had to spare.

As she furrowed her brow at the cryptic timetable, a sound drifted across from the beach: a long, drawn-out groan. Blair froze, a shiver travelling over her skin.

Then the groan came again, and something clicked in her mind: it was just a cow mooing. But now that she thought about it, Blair couldn't remember seeing a single cow since they'd arrived on the island. She'd only noticed a couple of small farms, with higgledy-piggledy fences surrounding a handful of sheep and chickens.

Then: a sparkle in the air, a cluster of light that vanished as quickly as it had come. Just like the light she had seen on the hillside yesterday. What had that boy called it? A will-o'-the-wisp. Or phosphorescence caused by something-or-other.

She shook her head and turned back to the road with a sigh. There was no time to lose. If she missed the morning ferry, it was all over. The next one wouldn't be until the evening, and then she'd miss the connecting train, and there wouldn't be another until the next day. She wasn't about to spend the night in a train station.

But the bellow returned, louder and more urgent than before. Blair reacted to the creature's distress without thinking, setting down her bike and skimming down the sandy soil of the short cliffside to the pebbled shore.

Blair turned on the spot, peering into the gloom. She blinked against another twinkle of white light and then, just ahead of her through the mist, she saw it.

It was a cow after all, but only a young one. The creature was no taller than her waist, with a broad, guileless face and wide nostrils that flared when it caught sight of her. It tried to buck, but it stumbled – it was caught on something.

Blair took a step towards it to get a closer look. There was some kind of webbing wrapped around its front legs, cutting into its flesh.

A fishing net.

She took another step and the calf snorted, eyes rolling in fear so that the whites flashed at her.

Blair crouched down and edged forwards, making soothing noises. But as her eyes roved over the creature her breath caught.

Its fur... She had thought it was a Highland cow, like they had on all the Scottish postcards. But up close, she realised it didn't have fur at all. It looked like seaweed: amber-coloured, curling and wet, like the orange stuff that was washed up all over the beach.

There was a warning note when the calf snorted again. Its gaze stayed locked onto Blair as she reached towards it. She laid a trembling hand flat against one of its front legs; the fur there was slippery and cool.

It *was* seaweed.

The calf stayed motionless, but its breath gusted over her head; it smelled briny. The animal made a half-hearted attempt to throw its weight backwards, but the net only pulled tighter. Blair could see that the net had become wedged beneath one of the rocks, and though it was battered and full of holes, the knots were still strong.

Carefully, she began to unwind the net from around the first leg. Coaxing the creature to lift its leg and place its cloven hoof in her palm took the longest, but then she was able to pull the knot free. She reached out to the other leg and did the same, but the final loop was tight. She picked up a sharp-edged stone near her foot and began to saw it away.

The net snapped suddenly, but the calf didn't seem to realise it was free. Blair put the pebble down and backed off, and at her movement the creature jolted, finally understanding that it wasn't stuck any more. It locked eyes with her again, then turned and loped away.

A satisfied smile broke out on Blair's face as it ran. The fog had almost lifted, and she expected to watch it gallop down the shore, over the road, back to wherever the rest of its herd was. But to her astonishment it made straight for the water. When its hooves struck the sea, it didn't hesitate. It only barrelled onwards with another bellow that was silenced when it vanished beneath the waves.

Blair glanced wildly over each shoulder, searching for another witness to this strangeness, but there wasn't a soul in sight.

She held her breath.

The calf didn't resurface.

Blair laughed uncertainly, feeling like the butt of a joke, then stopped short and frowned.

She had just seen a calf disappear into the sea. A calf with seaweed instead of fur.

And the lights that had beckoned to her... *will-o'-the-wisps*.

What exactly was happening here?

Something drifted into her line of sight, emerging from the mist into a patch of bright sunlight. It was the boxy shape of the ferry, heading for the harbour.

Blair's heart leapt into her mouth as she clambered back up the cliff. Her bike still lay where she'd left it, and she jumped on and set off down the road as fast as she could go.

She came rocketing into the harbour just as the ferry was pulling away from the dock. The fog had finally lifted, and the sky was so clear she couldn't quite tell where it ended and the sea began. Her shoulders slumped as the ferry drifted off into the blue haze.

"No need to look so forlorn, lass," said a man in a yellow mackintosh as he wound in ropes from the water. "They always come back."

Blair groaned. "It'll be too late by then."

Her phone was suddenly alive in her pocket. She pulled

it out and gasped – a bar of signal had somehow found her once again, and her phone was buzzing continuously as the protest planning chat updated with dozens upon dozens of messages.

A message popped up on the screen from Libby and she clicked it at once.

It was a selfie of her best friend, beaming in her heart-shaped sunglasses, captioned:

> can't wait to see you tomorrow!

Blair's hands tightened on the phone. She watched through teary eyes as the ferry drifted away, along with her hopes.

AN OLD REFRAIN

The house was still as Blair returned. She left the bike leaning on the garden wall and padded reluctantly up to the front door. There was no one in the kitchen, so she breathed a sigh of relief and crossed the room to her door, unzipping her bag as she went.

In her doorway she came to an abrupt stop. The room was brighter than she remembered it, because the hulking old wardrobe that had taken up the far wall was now lying on the floor in pieces. Her mum was in dungarees, humming as she used a flat tool to smooth the wall over.

Blair realised with a start that the hole in the wall where the baby bird had been nesting was gone. Filled in with plaster.

"What happened to the nest?" Blair asked, dropping her backpack to the floor.

Her mum started. "Blair, you scared me! You mean that pile of grass and feathers? I threw it away."

"What?! Mum, there was a baby bird inside!"

Her mum flushed crimson. "The nest was empty, I'm sure of it!" But there was a crease of doubt between her brows.

"I saw it this morning, Mum. It must be stuck outside… Nowhere to go, nowhere for its parents to come back to…" Blair's mind raced. She hadn't been gone that long; she could still save it.

"How was I to know? It looked abandoned! And we can't exactly have birds nesting in your bedroom!"

Blair shook her head. "I've got to find it. The poor thing!"

She ran from the room, out the back door and through the garden. She could see the crack in the wall where it had been plastered from the other side, and the debris of the nest on the ground. She dug through the remains, but there was no sign of the little creature. It wasn't hiding in the brambles; Blair cut her arms on the thorns in search of it.

Surely it couldn't have got any further. It still didn't have proper feathers; it couldn't fly. How could it possibly survive?

When Blair finally returned to her bedroom she opened her mouth to confront her mum, but stopped short. Her mum was already staring white-faced at her, Blair's open backpack in her hands.

"Where were you going with all these clothes?" she asked, but she carried on digging through the bag's contents, and suddenly went very still. Her hand came slowly out of the backpack, clasping a handful of creased twenty pound notes.

By the time her father entered the kitchen, Blair guessed that her mum was about midway through her rant. It had been going on for several minutes now, and as usual, it had taken her dad this long to get his nose out of whatever book he had been reading and make an appearance.

"—shows me that you have absolutely NO understanding of how hard we worked to get where we are, all our lives, scrimping and saving so that one day we could come here and YOU could grow up in a place that—"

"Hey, hey!" her dad soothed. "What's happened? Anna – kochanie – can we please talk in the hallway?"

Blair's mum took his arm and pulled him out of the room, slamming the door closed behind her. Blair strained her ears but heard only angry whispers, mixed with her dad's level murmur. She felt strangely calm. She didn't know what they could do to punish her that was worse than what they'd already done by bringing her here.

A few moments later her parents returned, sitting down opposite her at the table.

Her dad fixed her with an earnest gaze. "Were you trying to run away?" he asked.

Blair shook her head firmly. "I was only going to stay with Libby for two nights. So I could go to a meeting. That's all."

"Are you kidding me? You were running away from Roscoe to go to a *meeting*?" Her mum threw her hands in the air. "You're thirteen years old – you can't travel across the country on your own! Anything could have happened!"

Blair gritted her teeth, but her dad didn't join in. "You must miss your friends very much," he said evenly.

Blair was furious with her eyes at that moment for filling with tears. She didn't look at him.

"You know, Libby can come and visit us whenever she likes. And when school starts, you'll make new friends."

Blair squeezed her eyes shut and a few tears escaped. "No, I won't!" she burst out. "You don't understand, Tata. There's, like, *one* other kid in this stupid place and he already called me an incomer. I don't know what that means but I don't think it was a compliment! He didn't even care about the school strikes."

"It hurts us that you would try to run away, Blair," her dad said. "Can you see that? You know we've always dreamed of moving to *the legendary isle of Roscoe!*" It was an old refrain and her dad knew it, so he said it with a smile. But his face fell as he continued. "You knew this move was coming."

Blair swallowed, struggling to gather her thoughts. "My whole life is in Carlisle. There's no internet here, no signal… I can't even message anyone. How am I supposed to know what's going on? How am I supposed to *do* anything?"

There was a troubled dimple in her dad's chin, but he reached across the table and slid her phone towards him. "Maybe it will be good for you not to read the news so much for a little while," he said gently.

Blair felt her eyes brimming again as he tucked the phone into his pocket. She couldn't even find the words to protest.

Her mum put the wad of money onto the table, then folded her arms. Her dad clasped his hands and tried to meet Blair's eye, but she pretended not to notice.

"Your mum and I worked very hard for every pound here. You must not have realised that, or I know you wouldn't have taken it."

Blair stared at the money until it blurred and didn't look like anything at all. "I just want to go home," she said in a small voice.

Her dad sighed. "This is your home now, myszka."

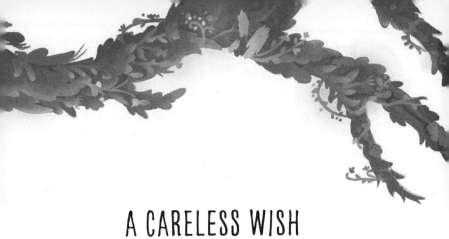

A CARELESS WISH

Angry tears prickled at Blair's eyes as she stormed up the hill. She'd only been in this quiet, lonely place a couple of days, but she already felt cut off. Far from her friends and their plans, the only things in the world that made her feel like everything might just be okay.

She turned her face into the wind and let it whip her hair away, steal the words from her mouth.

"I want to go home," she muttered. "I want to go home, I want to go home."

She stopped beside the standing stone. The sky had turned grey as smoke, the colours of the island muted and bleak.

"I wish I could go home," she whispered.

"It isn't an easy place to get used to," came the reply.

Blair almost jumped out of her skin. She wheeled around, certain she had been alone.

The voice belonged to a woman – taller than either of her parents, one of the tallest people Blair had ever seen.

She stood with her legs apart and her chin raised. Her wild hair hung almost to her waist, and from the crown of her head rose a pair of – antlers? Blair squinted at them, wondering how the woman had fastened them to her head, but they disappeared into her hair at the base.

She was smiling at Blair, and while it wasn't an unpleasant smile, there was something unnerving about it.

"Thanks," Blair said slowly. "I'll keep that in mind." She skirted around the woman. If there was one thing she knew from growing up in a city, it was never to talk to strangers who showed a bit too much interest in you.

Her heart sped up a little as the stranger fell into step beside her.

"You wish to go home?" the woman said.

Even though Blair was walking as quickly as she could, the woman was easily keeping pace, her long strides eating up the ground.

"I was just talking to myself."

"You should never make a wish carelessly," the woman scolded. Her voice was commanding and resonant. "Didn't your parents tell you that?"

"I don't think they believe in that sort of thing…" Exasperation was beginning to creep in alongside Blair's panic now – didn't they understand personal space on this island?

"You haven't met my kind before?" the woman asked curiously.

Blair could feel the chill of the wind that cut across from the ocean to the west, but when she glanced sidelong at the woman she saw that she wore only a sleeveless dress the deep red hue of rust, belted at her waist with cord, ragged around her ankles. She wasn't wearing shoes!

"Um, yeah, there were people like you on the mainland," Blair said. Facing forward again, she mouthed, "*Weirdos!*"

"Oh," the woman pondered. "I thought they had all moved on from Carlisle."

Blair stopped short. This wasn't right… She turned to the woman, who came to a stop a few feet from her. "How do you know where we're from?"

"Word travels fast on a small island," the woman said, with another one of those slightly creepy smiles. It was impossible to guess her age. Though her copper skin was unwrinkled, her cheeks were hollow and her eyes sharp. Her irises were a washed-out electric blue.

"I only want to make you an offer," the stranger said.

Blair huffed out a breath, unsure what she could say to shake her off. The more the stranger persisted, the more her heart quickened. But then she realised that over the woman's shoulder she could see the misshapen lump of their new house. She felt a stab of relief.

"My parents did teach me some things," she said. "Like not to talk to strangers."

She marched past the woman in the direction of the house.

The woman's voice echoed after her. "You want to go home. I can make your parents pick up and leave with a click of my fingers."

Blair hovered over her next step.

"Blair," the woman said, so sharply that Blair couldn't help but look. Had she told the woman her name? "Look around you," she commanded.

Some part of her wanted to know. Uncertainly at first, Blair glanced from side to side along the slopes of the hill.

Everywhere she looked, there were deer. Some with antlers, some without, old and young, in groups or alone. They were scattered all over the hillside, and every last one of them was looking her way: head raised, eyes fixed on the two of them.

"Nothing on Roscoe is what it seems," the woman said. "Granting your wish would be easy."

She beckoned with a finger and one of the animals began to move towards them: a young deer that walked up to Blair as bold as anything. Blair's eyes widened as she sank down into a crouch to look the creature in the eye. She reached out, and the fawn stayed still as her fingers brushed the soft fur of its neck and speckled back. She withdrew her hand and it trotted quickly back to its mother, who drew it close, sniffing its fur.

Blair straightened up. Her mouth felt dry. "Who are you?" she croaked.

"Cailleach Mho'r Nam Fiadh," came the woman's answer. "But Cailleach will do."

"KAL-yuch?" Blair repeated, trying to sound it out, but she couldn't picture the letters. It must be one of those tricky Gaelic spellings. She glanced again at the two great antlers balanced on Cailleach's head, but still she couldn't see how they were attached. They were white bone, not soft and velvety-looking like those of the stags around her.

With a shiver, Blair remembered the strange figure she thought she'd seen on the hillside on the day they'd arrived on Roscoe, illuminated by lightning – and the creeping feeling that she was being watched.

"What do you mean – that nothing is as it seems here?" she asked.

"You've noticed?" Cailleach said with a wry smile. "Look around. Tell me what you see."

Blair pushed her glasses up her nose to scan the area. Not one of the hills was large enough to be called a mountain, and the island was small enough that from their vantage point she could see graphite-grey sea in almost every direction. The hills themselves were a patchwork of yellow-flowering gorse, pink and purple heather, long grasses and dark strands of trees.

Though the sky had darkened since the morning, the flower meadows that bordered the shore around her house glittered as though still covered in dew. "A whole load of flowers," Blair said.

"Yes," Cailleach said. "We call it the machair."

That didn't seem to be the answer she was waiting for, though. There were small birds racing over the machair, seagulls wheeling over the harbour, and something big soaring over the hills. "Birds," Blair offered. "Deer, obviously..."

Cailleach nodded, expectant. Blair wondered where this guessing game was going. "The village." Was it her imagination, or did Cailleach flinch at the mention of it?

Blair noticed a shining silver ribbon running down from the hills into the village, where she could just about make out a bridge. Now that she'd noticed it, there were dozens of small tributaries leading into it, light glinting off their surfaces. "There's a river… streams, bogs… and the Atlantic, can't miss that." She frowned at a distant mirror gleam. "And a loch, I think? Lots of water, basically."

"Exactly." The tension seemed to ease out of Cailleach as she smiled. "A hundred miles from the mainland, half in the sea, half out of it. The rules are different here. Roscoe, you see, is one of the last places in the world where the human and fey realms still overlap."

Human and fey? Before Blair had a chance to process this statement, Cailleach began to stroll away across the hill. Blair hesitated. If she wanted to run, this was her chance. But instead she found herself hurrying after the strange woman, rolling Cailleach's words around in her mind.

"What do you mean, 'the fey realm'? What are fey?" she asked.

"We have been called many names. Fairies, the Sìth, the Guid Folk, the Still Folk, Seelie and Unseelie. There are as many kinds of fey folk as there are mundane creatures in your world. I myself am a guardian: we protect the rivers, trees, plants and animals. All living things have a guardian, and it has been my task to watch over the red deer of Roscoe."

For how long? Blair couldn't help but wonder.

"This world is our home, as it is yours, but where

human belief has dwindled, the fey realm has moved further and further away, until you could stand side by side with a redcap in the ruins of a castle and never know he was there. But not on Roscoe. Here, we still have a toehold in the realm of people."

Against her better judgement, Blair felt a surge of wonder. Could it really be true? Magic was something she'd stopped believing in a long time ago, around the time she'd started to understand what was happening to the planet. But there was no denying that there was something otherworldly about Cailleach and the magnetic pull she seemed to have over the deer.

Cailleach's meandering path brought them into a herd of the animals. Not one of them startled, not even at Blair's presence. One by one, russet-brown heads lifted to meet Cailleach's hand as she passed, like a queen greeting her people.

"The fey folk have many abilities," Cailleach said, nodding her head to acknowledge the broad-antlered stag standing sentinel at the edge of the group. She looked over her shoulder at Blair. "I believe I can convince your parents to take you home."

Blair felt her suspicions rise. "But why would you do that?"

Cailleach tilted her head, continuing her rounds. "We would be helping one another. You see, Roscoe has been out of balance for some time. Once I had a counterpart: his name was Bodach. Together, we protected the deer and the island that is their home. But in a time of great change, Bodach abandoned us. I have been trying to protect Roscoe alone ever since."

Blair wasn't quite sure what Cailleach meant about *balance*, but the guardian was still speaking.

"As you must have noticed, deer far outnumber almost any other species on Roscoe. That gives me a level of responsibility somewhat… *greater* than the other fey folk who inhabit this island. I try to look out for them where I can. However, there are places I cannot go, things I cannot do. Perform a few tasks to help me and my kin, and I will grant your wish."

Blair realised she should have known better than to expect something for nothing. Still, it was an alarming thought. She was just an ordinary girl. What could she possibly do to help someone magical? But if all Cailleach needed was a human, she supposed she was qualified.

"How many tasks?" Blair asked.

"Three is the traditional number," Cailleach answered without pause.

"Three tasks to help the fey folk…" Blair mused. "And you really think you can persuade my parents?"

Cailleach turned to face Blair, meeting her eyes with cold assurance. "I swear I will make them leave." Slowly, she extended her hand. "Do we have an agreement?"

Blair hesitated. She didn't exactly trust this woman, but what choice did she have? She glanced down the valley, to the ramshackle house at the end of the road. She knew she would never convince her parents to take her home. And staying here, cut off from everyone she knew, disconnected from the rest of the world … that was out of the question.

She took Cailleach's hand and shook it once, firmly. "All right," she said.

She made to withdraw her hand, but Cailleach's fingers gripped hers tightly. Her eyes gleamed and Blair jumped as something smooth and cold wound its way around her wrist like a snake. It was bone. It was … antler. It locked their hands together, tines unfurling, and then it ground to a stop.

"Your first task, then," said Cailleach. "A kelpie has been preying on my deer. Find it and do away with it. Once it is dealt with, return here."

Blair gaped at the antler binding her wrist to Cailleach's, and then before her eyes, it split in two: one bone bracelet around each of their wrists. Cailleach's dissolved into nothing, but Blair's remained in place, heavy and solid.

Cailleach's mouth curled at one corner. Then she released Blair's hand and walked swiftly away.

"Wait!" Blair called, rousing her stunned body into motion. "What's a kelpie?"

She ran after Cailleach, but the guardian passed beyond the standing stone. By the time Blair reached it, Cailleach was gone.

MAINLAND SPY

In the morning, Blair was woken by a familiar chirping sound. Her first instinct was to reach blearily for her phone, so she patted the bed around her and felt along the windowsill without lifting her head. Only when her search turned up nothing did she remember that her phone had been confiscated.

Which meant the chirping hadn't been her phone at all. She sat bolt upright, ears pricked.

Cheep!

Blair jumped to her feet and pushed open the window.

Cheep!

She stuck her head out, scanning the long grass directly beneath.

A pair of round, violet eyes stared back at her.

"You're alive!" Blair cried in relief. Not only was the little bird alive, it looked bigger and healthier than ever. Most of its body was covered in downy feathers, and it was definitely larger than when she'd last seen it – had that only been yesterday? It was filling out, becoming less of a blob and more of a ball, two sets of claws sticking out beneath the fluff.

"Are you all right down there?" Blair asked, but it was obvious that it didn't need help. Either the bird or its parents had furrowed a good hollow into the mossy ground, just big enough for its little round body. Tucked into the long grass beneath the wall, Blair suspected it would be invisible from anywhere but directly overhead.

The bird chirped happily again.

"Don't worry. I'll be here. If you need anything, just let me know."

She smiled at the little creature, ducked back into the room and pulled the window closed.

The door to her bedroom opened at once to reveal Blair's mum on the other side, one hand on her hip.

"Ever heard of knocking?" Blair grumbled.

"Who were you talking to?" her mum demanded.

"I don't have a secret phone, if that's what you're trying to say. Search my room if you want."

Blair's mum pursed her lips, as though that were a silly suggestion, but Blair suspected she was considering it.

"Get dressed. We're going to visit Morag's B&B."

"Why do I have to—"

The door closed before she'd even finished speaking.

Blair stood there silently fuming for a moment, then reluctantly started to get ready.

When she'd returned from the hills the night before, she'd searched all the boxes of books in their future sitting room, hoping to find something about mythical creatures. All her dad had were swashbuckling historical adventures and dog-eared sci-fi paperbacks.

She was no closer to finding out what a kelpie was. She'd intended to use the day to find a way to do some research, but now her mum had thrown another spanner in the works.

As the Zielinskis' battered yellow hatchback bumped along the road towards the village, Blair stared out of the passenger seat window. Her mind was far across the sea and back in time, to that day almost two years ago when she had been sitting alone at lunchtime on the first day of secondary school. She had seen Libby from across the playground, with her wide smile and her black locs, speaking animatedly to the kids around her. And this girl, who was far too cool to be interested in hanging out with Blair, had caught her eye and waved her over.

That lunchtime Blair had heard, for the first time, someone her own age talking passionately about the climate crisis, encouraging the others to come up with ideas for what they could do. When Blair had suggested they refuse to go to school – if she was being totally honest, it was a joke – Libby's eyes had lit up and she'd hugged Blair and started planning at once.

As she relived those moments, Blair twisted the antler around her wrist. Its solidity was discomfiting, and it smelled faintly of decay.

"Where did you get that bracelet?" her mum asked, frowning at it. "I've never seen it before."

"I… found it," Blair mumbled, unable to find the energy to come up with a decent lie. Her mum would find a reason to be angry regardless.

"What is it made of? It looks like – oh, yuck, like bone or something."

They pulled into the driveway of a long stone building with a fresh, neat coat of white paint. The clutch groaned as Blair's mum yanked it into place and turned off the engine.

"You shouldn't wear things you just find in the street," she grumbled. "You don't know where it's been."

Blair pushed the bracelet back into the sleeve of her jumper and followed her mum up to the purple front door. A sign hanging overhead pronounced it:

Fraoch
Guest House

A smaller sign in the window, backed by white net curtain, declared: VACANCIES.

The front door swung open before they had a chance to knock. Morag's broad-shouldered form filled the doorway in her chair, more so when she threw her arms wide.

"Welcome, welcome!" she proclaimed. "Welcome to Fraoch. Come right in."

Blair trailed behind her mum as they stepped into the warmth of the guest house. The walls were covered in framed photos, drawings and paintings, with one common theme – the Roscoe red deer. A fawn drinking from a river, a stag standing majestically on a hilltop, a herd galloping across a moor.

"We're almost fully booked for the festival already," Morag was saying. "I might be sending some business your way sooner than expected! Now, let's start with one of the bedrooms so you can see what the guests see when they arrive – it's all on theme, of course…"

Morag wheeled down the hallway to the first door on the left and led the way inside. Blair was the last to squeeze into the cosy room with a tartan-draped four-poster bed. Above the bed were a huge pair of antlers, which Blair stared at in alarm.

"Not to worry," Morag chuckled, following Blair's gaze. "The stags shed their antlers every year. Mother found those in the hills. Now Anna, I've a funny story about the choice of tartan for the hangings…"

Blair couldn't even pretend to be interested, so after a few moments she walked silently out of the room. Her mum and Morag seemed to be too deep in conversation to notice.

Blair glanced around. The hallway snaked off in both directions, lined with identical white doors. But under the stairs was a small alcove with a desktop computer. Blair's eyes widened. Quickly, she slid into the seat and moved the mouse.

The computer woke up. There was no password. It was connected to the internet.

Blair couldn't believe her luck.

She opened a private browser and logged into her messages as speedily as she could. She already had a dozen, but the group chat was busy – the meeting was happening *right now*. There were pictures of the sketches for the skeleton puppets they were going to build.

A new photo popped up. It was a group shot of everyone at the meeting – basically every one of Blair's friends, with Libby front and centre.

The only person missing was Blair. But it didn't look like they'd even noticed.

Blair's chest clenched painfully.

The bedroom door handle began to rattle. Heart racing, Blair closed the browser and darted up the narrow stairs, ignoring the sign that read: **Private**.

From the landing, she heard Morag and her mum leaving the room and moving on to the next. The door closed, and Blair let out a breath.

Suddenly she realised she had missed a perfect opportunity. She had been *on a computer* – she could have easily searched for information about kelpies, but instead all she'd done was made herself feel even worse.

She was drawn out of these thoughts by a tuneful sound behind her – someone was humming.

"Ouch!" The humming stopped as the singer hissed. Then there was a sigh, and it picked up again.

Blair turned around. There were two doors on the

landing: one was wide open to a bathroom, and the other was ajar, a crack of light striping the carpet.

Blair peeked through the gap into a bright room, where the grey light of the sea and sky streamed in through a huge window. In front of the window was a workbench big enough to seat eight for dinner, and every inch of it was covered in hand tools, scraps of fabric and balls of yarn. An old woman with hazel skin and long white hair gathered in a ponytail sat hunched over the table, wearing a rainbow-striped woollen jumper. As Blair watched, she stabbed a huge needle mercilessly and repeatedly into what looked like a ball of wool. She flinched with a hiss and cried again, "Ouch!"

Startled, Blair shifted in the doorway and the door creaked open. The old woman's flinty eyes caught hers at once.

"I think you've wandered the wrong way, my dear," she said. "The rooms are back down the stairs."

The smile faded from Blair's face. "I'm not staying here."

The woman's eyes narrowed. "You must be a mainland spy, then."

Blair opened her mouth to respond, but now that the door had swung wide, every detail of the colourful room was suddenly on display. The marine-blue walls were covered with a patchwork of crafts: tapestries, watercolours, embroidery, crochet, quilts, clay creations and mosaics. Shelves all around the room were cluttered with wool and needles, paints, pencils, pastels, charcoal, pots and canvases. A narrow single bed stood in the corner, but it was more gallery than bedroom.

In the centre of the workbench was a basket full of different-coloured tufts of wool, and a piece of cork pierced with several long needles. Directly in front of the old woman was a big square of foam, on which the wool had been artfully arranged into a picture.

"What are you doing?" Blair asked, her interest piqued.

"Who are you?" the woman countered.

"Blair Zielinski," she answered. "My parents bought the house at the end of the road."

The woman regarded her shrewdly for a moment longer, then gestured with a wave to the seat beside her.

"Pull up a chair."

Blair didn't need to be told twice. She perched on the seat she was offered and watched keenly as the old woman positioned her lump of reddish-brown wool on the square of foam. Now that it was in front of her, Blair could see a landscape taking shape: a sunset of swirling pink and gold over the hills. The brown lump seemed to be a deer.

The woman handed the needle to Blair; it looked big enough to be a murder weapon. "You can attach the deer to the background by poking it with this. It's best to do small, quick motions."

Blair held the needle over the helpless creature, uncertain.

"Now stab it," the old woman encouraged her. "Just keep stabbing it."

Blair did as she was told, poking the needle quickly in and out of the animal shape. She felt it starting to catch on the wool beneath, and the 3D deer began to flatten onto the backdrop. "This is cool!"

"This is needle felting," the old woman said, a wry smile on her face.

Blair's hand started to ache. She paused to rub it. "Are you Morag's mother?" she asked.

The woman chuckled. "Aye. My name's Rosemary."

The room filled suddenly with the sound of rain hammering on glass, and Blair saw that the steely skies had finally let loose. Through the blur of splattering raindrops on the window she could see the slate rooftops of what looked like the whole village, and beyond it the sea, stretching out to the sky far beyond. On a day like this, you couldn't even see the giant shadow of the nearest island, thirty miles away. Roscoe could have been alone in the world.

"You have a good view from here," she remarked.

"Aye, if you like the ocean," Rosemary agreed, taking the needle from Blair. She picked up where she had left off.

"So do you?" Blair pulled a small piece of black wool from the basket and set it near the top of the image, in the rough v-shape of a bird in flight.

"Roscoe would be the wrong place to be living if I didn't." Rosemary assessed Blair's suggestion for a moment, then nodded once. Pleased with herself, Blair plucked another of the needles from the cork and began to poke her bird into place in the sky.

Soon she forgot all of the urgency and frustration she'd been feeling since her meeting with Cailleach. They worked in silence for a while; Blair could hear the rolling of Morag's wheels and her mum's footsteps beneath them, doors opening and closing, low voices.

This bright, busy room was such a contrast to the B&B downstairs. There seemed to be no craft Rosemary hadn't turned her hand to. Blair gazed around, noticing that the collection of artworks depicted scenes as well as landscapes. Creatures below ground and in the eaves of houses, people transforming into animals and trees...

"Is that a sketchbook?"

The question startled her. She saw that Rosemary was gesturing towards her half-open backpack, discarded beside the chair. Poking out of it was the spiral-bound corner of her current sketchbook.

Blair glanced over at the old woman in the heart of her studio, surrounded by her collected works. "Do you want to see?"

In answer, Rosemary held out her hands. Blair placed the book carefully into them. The only person she had ever let look through her sketchbooks before was Libby.

Blair fiddled with a piece of wool while Rosemary leafed through, pretending to continue their work, though it was impossible to concentrate. Rosemary was looking at the deer Blair had sketched on the hilltop; then she turned the page and hovered over an illustration of the calf on the beach at sunrise.

"Fairy cattle," Rosemary muttered.

"What?" Blair asked at once.

Rosemary held up the drawing. "Fairy cattle. Sea cows

that come ashore to graze at night and disappear with the dawn. See how they've coats of orange kelp?" Rosemary tapped her fingers against the slick curls of the cow's fur.

Blair's heart stuttered. She remembered the slippery feeling of the kelp beneath her fingers so vividly, the sea-salt smell of the calf's breath. "Is that what it is?"

Rosemary watched her for a moment. "That's what some folk call them. Their true name's crodh mara."

Did that mean this woman knew the truth about this island? Blair looked across at her, eyes alight, a hundred questions jumping to her lips.

Rosemary closed the sketchbook and handed it back to Blair.

"I don't suppose you know what a kelpie is?" Blair ventured.

Rosemary frowned. "Why'd you want to know about those shapeshifters?"

Blair's heart leapt. *Shapeshifters*! But she shrugged nonchalantly, trying not to give anything away. She pulled a piece of soft, lavender wool from the basket and held it up to the light, but her sleeve rolled down, revealing the antler bracelet clasped around her wrist. She dropped the wool and swiftly pulled her sleeve back up. "Someone mentioned it to me," she said quickly.

Rosemary's gaze seemed to be fixed on her sleeve. When they returned to Blair's face, the old woman's eyes were sharp. "Why didn't you ask them?"

Blair just shrugged again. Rosemary sighed and pushed her stool back from the table; Blair saw with alarm that there was a tremor in her hands. The old woman stretched and bent her fingers a few times, watching Blair with a strange wariness.

"Roscoe is the furthest island from the mainland, all alone at the edge of the silver sea. In a place like this, my dear, anything could happen."

SHAPESHIFTERS

"Mother, do you have a hostage up there?" came a voice from the bottom of the stairs.

The far-off look on Rosemary's face faded away, replaced by a weary amusement. "Here comes the cavalry." She beckoned with a jerk of her head for Blair to follow her out of the room.

Rosemary stopped on the landing; Morag and Blair's mum were stationed at the foot of the stairs. "I had a visitor," the old woman said, prodding Blair in the back. "She was just leaving."

"I'm so sorry," Blair's mum gushed. "Blair, get down here! What were you doing, sneaking around?"

Blair moved reluctantly down the stairs. "Rosemary is an *artist* and she was *teaching* me to needle felt."

"Oh, are you an artsy type as well? How lovely!" Morag said delightedly. "Perhaps you could come and have a crafternoon with Mother from time to time? Her hands aren't what they used to be, and I'm sure she'd love the company! What do you think?"

Blair wasn't quite sure what to say; she looked to the old woman for help. Rosemary's face was half in shadow, but after a moment, she shifted into the light.

"Aye. Let the girl come, if she'd like to."

"She'd love to. Wouldn't you, Blair?"

Since there was apparently no need for her to say anything, Blair just nodded.

"Right, then!" Morag spun on the spot and waved them towards the door. Blair followed last; Rosemary nodded to her and disappeared back into her room.

"...think I might even get a swim in this evening!" Blair's mum was saying, and Morag looked back over her shoulder, aghast.

"Swimming! In the sea, you mean?"

"Of course!"

"Well, all I can say is, you're mad. Not least because it's cold. You've got to be careful in the twilight hours on Roscoe... The island's haunted, you see."

"Haunted!" Blair's mum laughed, then stopped short when she realised Morag was straight-faced. Blair stepped closer, intrigued.

"That's right," Morag said, seeming to relish their attention. "By a monstrous shapeshifter. On Roscoe, in the witching hours between day and night, farm animals go missing... pets are never seen again... and bad things happen to people caught out in the hills. Swim if you must, but never at the new moon. They say that's when the creature rises from the sea loch..."

71

"Sounds spooky," Blair's mum said, sounding distinctly un-spooked. But Blair's senses had all sharpened at the mention of the word *shapeshifter*.

"What's it called?" Blair asked.

"Some call it the Sea Stag, but its *true* name is the Fiadh Mho'r," Morag said, her eyes widening with every syllable. Clearly she expected some kind of gasp or shriek at this, but Blair just pursed her lips, feeling like a popped balloon. Not a kelpie, then.

"You should go to the pub across the road." Morag sat back in her chair, evidently disappointed by her audience. "Have a look at the Sea Stag Inn's stained glass windows. They tell the story."

"Maybe we will," Blair's mum said, and then they bade their farewells and were ushered out of the house. The calico cat that Blair had seen from the car on that first day was stalking a mouse in the flower bed outside, its tail flicking from side to side.

To Blair's surprise, her mum actually did start walking across the road. Fresh air eddied around them as they made their way to the pub. The rain had passed and now even the clouds were blowing away, revealing patches of blue sky.

The Sea Stag Inn sat on the corner of the main road and the cobbled harbour, and the sign hanging above the door depicted a pair of black antlers. Three windows in carved stone niches were set into the wall that faced the harbour. The first pane was missing and boarded up; the wood that had been used to cover it was damp and weathered, so it must have been missing for a while.

The second portrayed a man with his back to the viewer, stepping into the dark waters of a loch. The image had been constructed with fragments of coloured glass in a way that reminded Blair of the mosaics she'd seen on Rosemary's walls, but the pieces were joined with something liquid and silver. The waters were blue-black, and the hills on the distant shore were composed of purples and greens. The man's skin was bronze, his kilt a faded scarlet. But his feet didn't look quite right: bare and cloven and black. *Hooves.*

The third pane depicted the same view of the loch and the hills, but the hoofed man had vanished. A colossal creature was standing in the shallows in his place, its front hooves on the turf, its back legs half-submerged. It was a giant deer, its antlers so broad they almost filled the frame.

"I *love* local legends," Blair's mum said, peering at the final pane. "What do you think? He turns into the massive deer? What did Morag call it, the Fee-ugh Vore?"

"Something like that." Blair was only half-listening; the windows didn't shed any more light on her kelpie situation. She turned and looked back at the B&B, wondering if she should have pressed Rosemary further.

"Morag almost seemed like she really believed it!" Blair's mum said with a chuckle.

"Maybe she does," Blair replied. Her gaze drifted away from the B&B, a few doors down, to a very peculiar house.

It was a boat. It had been a big boat, once, but now it was a small house. The front door was set into the side, and the walls of the house curved to a prow at one end.

The upstairs windows were all portholes. With the guttering and the slate roof, Blair hadn't really noticed it when they'd driven past before. But now that she saw it whole, there was no ignoring it.

This was where that boy, Alasdair, had said he lived. *The boat house, opposite the general store.*

It had to be the one.

Alasdair had known about will-o'-the-wisps. Maybe he could tell her *something* about kelpies.

"I'm going to the shop. Blair, are you listening?" Her mum was speaking and she hadn't even realised.

"Sorry." Blair turned around. "Is it okay if I wait out here? I just want to go for a wander around."

Her mum looked cautiously pleased by this. "Of course you can. Don't go far, I won't be long." With that, she headed off to the general store, the bell tinkling as she entered.

Blair marched straight up to the front door of the boat house before she could change her mind. She forced herself to lift her fist and knock, reminding herself that this was her best chance of getting home.

There was silence for a moment, then the sound of footsteps approaching. The door swung open, and a woman stepped into the gap between the door and the frame, blocking the entrance. She had the same pale skin and snub nose as Alasdair, though her hair was dark and curly: this had to be his mum. Her face dropped into a frown when she saw Blair.

"Can I help you?"

"I'm looking for Alasdair," Blair said.

"He's not here." She moved to close the door.

"Where is he?" Blair asked quickly.

Alasdair's mum jerked her head in the direction of the hills behind the house. "Out there. Doing his deer survey, same as every day."

"Thanks," Blair said with a relieved smile. For some reason, Alasdair's mum now hovered for a moment with the door half-closed.

"What's your name?" she asked.

"Blair Zielinski."

"From the new family at the steading."

"Yeah."

The door closed abruptly in Blair's face.

Straight after lunch, Blair gathered her stuff together before she could be roped into jobs around the house. Her parents looked alarmed by her sudden determination to go out exploring, so Blair made a show of putting her sketchbook and markers into her backpack to give herself an alibi. She promised to be home by dinner and set off.

She knew it was a small island, but Roscoe seemed intimidatingly large as Blair hiked across the machair towards the hills. She was hopeful that, since she'd run into Alasdair near her house only a few days earlier, he'd still be in the area somewhere. After all, if he was being systematic about this survey business he'd be working his way around bit by bit.

Blair started by huffing and puffing her way to the standing stone at the top of the nearest hill, where she'd bumped into him on that awful day. The sky was clear today and the sun seemed to light every blade of grass that the breeze rustled through.

But Blair couldn't see another person anywhere, so she laboured up to the summit of the next highest hill, where she had to stop to catch her breath.

And then she saw him. Alasdair was crouched down in the heather, scribbling away at a clipboard propped on his knees. She steeled herself and trotted down the slope to meet him.

He didn't look up until she was almost upon him. Then he just screwed up his eyes and said, "Oh, it's you."

"Yes, it's me. Blair, remember?"

"I know. I wasn't trying to be rude the other day, you know."

Blair was surprised by this, but she wasn't going to let it show. "Calling me an incomer? Well, maybe you should consider how it might make someone feel before you say it next time."

He shrugged. "Aren't you going to apologise, too?"

Blair laughed in disbelief. "You *haven't* apologised. And what exactly am I supposed to apologise for? Do you understand that sea-level rise means the entire village will be underwater in a few decades if we don't do anything about it? Or are you not worried, since your house can float?"

She suppressed a smile, though she was quite pleased with that one.

Alasdair looked disgruntled, but not quite angry. "If you're not apologising, I'm not going to."

"That's fine." Blair folded her arms. "It's in the past, I don't care. But there was something I wanted to ask you, and your mum said you'd be out here."

Alasdair looked back at his clipboard and returned to scratching away with his pencil. It wasn't the most promising start, Blair had to admit. She sat down a few feet away, not wanting to crowd him.

"What are you writing?" she asked.

"Well, before you came thundering down here, there was a doe and a fawn on the ridgeline there." He pointed with the end of his pencil. "They're gone now." He cast a salty look her way. "But I'm writing down how many I saw, how old they might be, what sex they are and where I saw them."

"For the survey?" Blair asked, curiosity getting the better of her.

"That's right. For the Roscoe Biodiversity Trust. We monitor the deer numbers because we're trying to make sure that everything lives in balance, people and deer and all the other species. But the deer population has been increasing over the years, and they're overgrazing. You know how there are, like, hardly any young trees? Well, it's not supposed to be that way. The scientist who advises us even suggested we might introduce large predators. I'm the youth representative on the board." He stopped suddenly and flushed pink, like he hadn't intended to say so much.

"That's so cool," Blair said. It was.

"Thanks." Alasdair squinted at the page, avoiding her gaze. "Was that what you wanted to ask about?"

"Um, no." Blair shifted her weight. "You know those… will-o'-the-wisps?"

"The phosphorescence caused by escaping gas." Alasdair nodded.

"Sure. Well, since you knew about the… phosphorescence… I was wondering if you might know anything about kelpies."

He looked up from his work. "Water monsters," he said simply. "Shapeshifting creatures that take the form of horses on land to lure weary travellers onto their backs so they can drown and devour them. Are those the kelpies you mean?"

Blair blinked rapidly. The words *drown and devour* seemed to be caught on a loop in her mind. This was the first task Cailleach had given her? How on earth was she supposed to defeat a deadly monster that wanted to *drown and devour* her?

She took a deep breath, returning to reality. "Yes. I think so. Wait a minute." She dug her sketchbook out of her backpack and uncapped a marker. "Tell me everything you just said again, slowly."

Alasdair's brow creased, but he didn't argue with her. As he spoke, her hand darted across the white paper, leaving shining black lines in its wake.

"According to the legends, a kelpie is a water horse. But they aren't horses, not really. No one has ever seen a kelpie's true form and lived to tell the tale. They live in freshwater, and they take the shape of a horse on land. In the stories, tired travellers see a horse standing there and think, *Aha, I can ride home.* But the moment they climb on its back, the kelpie dives under the water with the unlucky traveller and eats them alive. Or drowns them. I'm not sure which comes first."

Blair flinched at this, but her hands were still busy when Alasdair finished speaking. Finally she capped her pen and held the sketchbook at arm's length to examine it. Alasdair leaned over to have a look.

Her drawing depicted a horse standing on a riverbank, looking straight at the viewer. Water dripped from its fur, riverweed was tangled in its mane and tail, and shells clung to its hooves. There was an expression of pure malice on its long face.

"Cool," Alasdair said, and despite the fact that it was the first kind word he'd said to her, Blair felt herself glowing with pride. But then she looked at her creation again and a feeling of dread crept along her limbs, seeping out to her fingers and toes. This creature was *her* problem.

"I don't suppose you know how to... get rid of them?"

Alasdair looked at her with an utterly baffled expression. "They aren't *real.*"

Blair bristled, though a few days earlier she would have said exactly the same thing. "Says who?"

"Science. Reason."

"Okay, sure. But you know the stories, right? Do *they* say anything about how to get rid of a kelpie? It doesn't sound like something you'd want hanging around."

Alasdair pondered for a moment. "The only version I can remember ends with the traveller getting dragged into the burn."

"The what?"

"*Burn*. A stream. Honestly, you are such an in— I mean, so English. Why do you want to know?"

Blair tucked her pen behind her ear, making a swift decision. "Because I've heard there's a kelpie on the island, and I'm going to find it."

Alasdair burst into laughter. "That's ridiculous. Where did you hear something like that? And what makes you think you'll be the one to find it?"

"So you *do* think there could be one!" Blair countered, and Alasdair stopped laughing abruptly.

"No. I think it's rubbish."

This boy was exhausting. "That's fine. I don't need you to believe me." Blair stood up, looking around. There was a small stream close by, running down to a shining bog; she began walking towards it. "You said they live in freshwater, right? So I'll check the bogs and streams. And the loch."

To her surprise, Alasdair followed her. "First of all, the loch's a sea loch. It's not freshwater. Secondly, there are about a hundred burns on this island. You'll never manage it all."

Blair inspected the dark, still water of the bog, but no horses came jumping out of it. "You manage to survey the whole island on your own, don't you? How hard can it be?"

Alasdair rolled his eyes. "It takes me the whole summer. Besides which, I have a map. You don't."

"Can I borrow yours?"

Alasdair drew his clipboard closer. "Obviously not. I need it."

He was still wearing the same holey, baggy fleece he'd been wearing when they first met. It reminded her of the old jumper of her dad's she liked to wear, and that endeared him to Blair, just a little bit. An idea occurred to her that she dismissed at once – but then she reconsidered. She didn't know her way around, and it *would* be nice to have company.

"What if we worked together?" she offered. "You could do your survey, and I could look for the kelpie."

He blinked, taken aback by the suggestion, and she couldn't blame him. "I mean… it would be good to have another pair of eyes. Even if you *are* on a completely pointless quest."

"Great!" Blair said quickly, before he could backtrack. "I'll meet you here tomorrow morning." She turned and began to jog away in the direction of the steading.

"You'll need some proper shoes!" Alasdair called after her. "Walking boots, if you have them. I don't want to get the blame if you die of hypothermia."

Blair looked down at her old trainers. They were soaked through. She hadn't even noticed.

THE VEINS
OF THE ISLAND

In the morning, Blair found her dad sitting at the kitchen table in his ancient striped dressing gown, sipping a cup of herbata while he read his book.

"Good morning, myszka. You're up early."

Blair adjusted her backpack on her shoulder. "Going out to draw before it rains." Her father raised his eyebrows and attempted to hide a smile, but not before she noticed. She grabbed a slice of bread from the loaf on the table and headed out before he could quiz her further.

By the time she reached the standing stone, Blair's feet were – miraculously – still dry. The night before, she'd dug out a pair of her mum's old work boots, and with a thick pair of woollen socks they were a decent fit. Alasdair had given her sound advice, even if he hadn't delivered it in the most helpful way. Prickly as he may be, Blair was relieved to be exploring the island with someone who actually knew their way around.

Alasdair was already standing atop the next summit, so

she jogged up to him, though it knocked the breath out of her. He was holding the promised map up in front of him and studying it closely. It was covered in handwritten notes and symbols, but they had been written in clever, winding ways that left nothing obscured.

Beneath Alasdair's scribblings, Blair saw that the island had the bent-oval shape of a kidney, with the hills running down the centre of it like a spine. They were labelled *The Creachanns*. The whole thing was criss-crossed with blue lines like a network of veins.

"That's a lot of water," Blair remarked. "You weren't joking."

"I never joke," Alasdair said, which Blair hoped *was* a joke. "I've already finished surveying the machair, so we'll head inland. I'll do my work, and you can do… yours. But you've got to be quiet so you don't spook the deer or this isn't going to work."

Blair mimed zipping her lips closed.

She followed in Alasdair's boot prints along the ridge. The sky was steel-grey, threatening rain. When they reached the next peak, Alasdair pointed at a thin blue line on the map, then gestured silently. Blair followed his outstretched finger and set off, doing her best to keep her footsteps quiet, but they seemed to squelch every other step in the soggy ground.

There was a herd of deer deep in the valley and Alasdair was already busy squinting at them through his binoculars and jotting things down. Blair consulted the map and then followed the curve of the hill around until she entered a small grove of trees, where she could hear the sound of trickling water.

A moment later, she came upon a small waterfall. Clear rivulets of water poured over slick, black rock into a still pool. Beads of moisture clung to the luminous green moss on the surrounding stones, and a narrow stream flowed away from the mouth of the pool, down the hillside.

There were no horses in sight, but just to be safe, Blair picked up a stone and cast it into the water. It sank with a *plop*, but no murderous shapeshifters emerged to drag her under.

As Blair stood at the water's edge, she began to notice a sound above the gentle tinkling of the stream. It sounded like a quiet voice – a woman's, perhaps. She was humming, or maybe… whimpering…

"*Blair…*" the voice whispered, but it rose almost to a sob as it repeated, "*Blair…*"

Blair felt the hairs on the back of her arms rise. She turned in a slow circle, but she could see no sign of anyone else in the grove. Yet there were footprints in the damp earth at the edge of the pool. No, not footprints – *pawprints…*

The voice seemed to echo around the trees, coming from everywhere and nowhere all at once. The shape of the word changed; it was not her name any more.

"*Beware…*"

Blair geared herself up to shout at the stranger to show themselves.

But then a shrill cry punctured the air – a shriek so piercing that the deer in the valley below scattered.

Blair's resolve evaporated at once; she sprinted to Alasdair without looking back.

He was already on his feet. "What are you shouting about?"

"It wasn't me!" Blair protested.

Her face must have been grey because Alasdair asked, "Are you okay?"

Blair pointed back where she'd come from. "There's something there."

Alasdair followed the line of her shaking finger. "It was just a fox," he assured her. "They make creepy sounds like that sometimes."

"There was a *voice*," Blair insisted. "It wasn't just the shriek. It was saying my *name*."

"Now you're just being silly," Alasdair said firmly.

Blair grabbed him by the arm and tugged him with her back to the grove. They walked slowly amongst the sparse hazel trees, whose prickly branches were encrusted with ghostly, pale green lichens.

A breeze rustled through the leaves, and then the whimpering returned.

Blair fought the urge to run. She looked at Alasdair instead; his eyes were wide, his jaw set.

"Is someone there?" Blair called tentatively.

"*Blair...*" the voice lamented again. "*Bewaaaaaaaare...*"

She shivered all over. Alasdair was frozen in place, and Blair knew he was hearing it too. But he seemed to have spotted something over her shoulder, and his brow furrowed.

Blair turned slowly on the spot.

There were sheets and shirts and other cloths hanging from the branches of a stunted hazel tree, dripping, as though they'd just been hung out to dry. But Blair hadn't seen them before – so where had they come from?

Alasdair moved to stand alongside Blair, swallowing audibly. "Bean Nighe," he murmured. "The washer-woman…"

The breeze picked up, sending the cloths fluttering wildly. The whimpering became a long, drawn-out groan, which grew into a howl. Alasdair seemed rooted to the spot.

A gust swept between the trees, brushing the back of Blair's neck. It seemed to slither down her arm and around her wrist, a cold flurry that rattled the antler bracelet.

"We're getting out of here." Blair grabbed Alasdair's hand and pulled him after her as she ran from the gloom of the hazel wood into the diffuse grey daylight.

When they were well out of sight of the pool, Alasdair dropped her hand. Blair was relieved to realise she couldn't feel that strange breath around her wrist any more.

"What's going on?" Alasdair demanded. "I've lived here all my life and *nothing* like that has ever happened to me. I'd never seen anything more exciting than a will-o'-the-wisp before you came along and started talking about kelpies, and now…"

"Now what?" Blair pushed, ignoring his questions. "What do you think that was? Who is the washerwoman?"

Alasdair sniffed, rubbing his arms as though still feeling

the chill of that otherworldly presence. "The Bean Nighe. They say she's half human, half fox. She sits on the banks of burns, weeping as she washes… If you hear her, it's a warning that something terrible is going to happen."

"But you don't believe any of that," Blair said, trying to reassure herself. "Science and reason, remember?"

"Of course not," he croaked.

Blair looked back the way they had come. "Maybe she wanted to warn us. About the kelpie."

Alasdair rolled his shoulders. "It was just some kind of… meteorological phenomenon. A small whirlwind. What we heard was probably the wind whistling through the rocks. It's funny really…"

He laughed weakly, but Blair wasn't convinced. He still looked a bit green around the gills.

Blair folded her arms. "The kelpie, the Bean Nighe – how do you know all this?"

"My granddad," he said. "I mean, I never met him. But he knew all these old folk songs, in Gaelic and English. My mum recorded them on a cassette tape before he died. I've listened to it a lot. My brother Ewan plays it constantly."

"A tape?" Blair repeated. "Retro."

To her surprise, Alasdair smiled. It brightened his face so completely that Blair was startled into smiling back.

They left the spooky pool behind them and walked through the day together, and the heavy clouds never quite broke. Everywhere they came upon herds of red deer, but nowhere did Blair see a horse.

They had run out of snacks and Blair's stomach was telling her it was time to go home. Alasdair seemed to feel the same, because he was packing his clipboard away.

"No sign of your kelpie yet," he remarked.

Blair grunted in frustration. "The streams are all too narrow and shallow. If you're going to capture a big animal and drag them into the depths, there have to be some depths to drag them into, right?"

Alasdair nodded slowly as he thought this over. "Sound reasoning. Some of the bogs around here are pretty deep. That's why you have to keep to the paths."

"*You* don't keep to the paths."

"I know this island inside out. Yet another reason you're so lucky I agreed to help you." There was a grin on Alasdair's face, daring Blair to rise to the bait.

Blair felt her face crease in an answering smile; for once, she didn't feel the urge to snap back at him. "Yeah, whatever. Tomorrow, I'm all about bogs."

"I can't wait to fish you out of them."

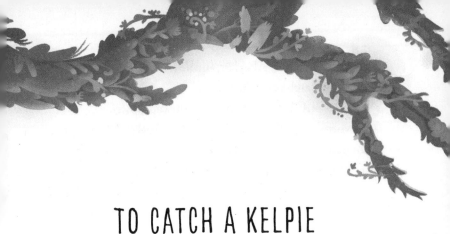

TO CATCH A KELPIE

In spite of their eerie encounter the day before, Alasdair was waiting for Blair in the same place the following morning.

"Still chasing fairy tales, then?" he asked.

"Of course. I've even got some unsuspecting bait to catch the kelpie." Blair raised her eyebrows pointedly.

They headed north rather than west this time, deeper into the heart of the island. While Alasdair took measurements and made notes, Blair paced around the edges of bogs. From time to time she noticed Alasdair looking her way, until she caught his eye – then he'd quickly get back to work.

Despite himself, he was curious.

She didn't feel quite at ease – not after the events of the day before – but the sun was shining and the sky was clear, and she kept an eye out for creepy laundry.

Blair felt herself becoming more adept at noticing the glint of sunlight on still water and identifying the clumps of reeds that liked the swampier areas. She began to range further from Alasdair, until she realised that he was jogging to catch up to her.

"Hang on!" he called, and she slowed down.

"Worried the kelpie's going to get me?" Blair teased, although as soon as the words were out of her mouth it occurred to her that she probably *shouldn't* have gone wandering off alone. The will-o'-the-wisps, the fairy cattle, the Bean Nighe... If they were all real, she really should be more wary of this killer horse.

Alasdair put his hands on his hips, out of breath. "I'm worried you'll get lost in the Creachanns and die of exposure, and I'll be held responsible."

"Sure," Blair began to say, but she went to take a step and found that there was nothing under her boot. She sank into bog up to her knee with a yelp.

To her surprise, instead of rolling around laughing, Alasdair reached out an arm to help her out. When they managed to get her free of the sucking bog, she found that her leg was coated in blackish mud.

"I think that makes you an official islander," Alasdair said. "It's a rite of passage."

"I'm so honoured," Blair said. The fetid smell of the bog mud was almost enough to make her gag.

She looked around. They were high on the plateau now, in a shallow bowl pocked with shining silver bogs. There were a few trees growing on the hummocks of land between the water, their leaves dark green and curling.

"What are these?" Blair asked, reaching for one of the waxy, yellow-edged leaves.

"Alders," Alasdair explained. "They love water. So naturally, they love Roscoe. There are no saplings, though – there are so many deer now, they eat the shoots before they can grow…" He paused, peering up into the branches. "Do you hear that?"

When she held still, Blair found that she *could* hear something – a kind of low, nasal hum that began to sound more and more like a growl.

Blair took a step back from the tree just as a lithe creature leapt down from the highest boughs to the branch right in front of them and hissed.

Alasdair tumbled backwards into the bog, sending up a splash. Blair flinched as bog-water rained down on her.

She leaned down to help haul Alasdair up. But there was a flash of movement beside her and she cried out as sharp claws sunk into her right arm, just above her antler bracelet. Blair swerved away, plunging sideways into the water. She sat up quickly, hardly noticing that her clothes were soaked through.

"What *is* that?"

The feline creature was hunched in front of them on the grassy hummock, hissing. It was thicker than a regular cat, with stripy markings on its tabby body. Its face was round and furry, more like a lion's than a house cat's, and its tail was bushy. The creature had a heavy brow, lending it an angry expression that was only heightened by the size of its teeth as it snarled.

"Wildcat," Alasdair answered, spitting reeds from his mouth.

"That is *not* a cat," Blair muttered.

"That's because they're native animals. They're not the same as domestic cats." Alasdair moved as though to get up but the cat lunged forwards, warning him away, and he sat back with a splash.

Blair made a snap decision and surged upright, yelling as loud as she could and sending water flying. The wildcat fled at the sudden movement, snaking back up the alder tree and disappearing into the leaves. Another noise drifted down from the boughs above, but this time it wasn't a hiss. It was a rising, braying meow that sounded uncannily like... laughter.

Alasdair pushed himself to his feet and gave Blair a hand up onto firm ground. In unspoken agreement, they moved quickly over the remainder of the bog and marched up the side of the bowl until they could look back down into it. There was no sign of the creature.

"Regular wildcats do *not* make sounds like that," Alasdair said. He didn't seem to know what to say next.

Blair raised her right arm to inspect the scratches around her wrist. They were only shallow, but one of the wildcat's claws had left a long gouge in the antler bracelet. "I wouldn't consider myself a cat person, but that thing definitely had it in for me."

"I don't remember any of Granddad's songs being about a magical wildcat... But if there's a Cù-Sìth, I suppose there could be a – a Cat-Sìth or something..."

"What's a Coo Shee?" Blair asked.

"A hellhound. According to legend, anyway. If he barks three times, it means—"

"Let me guess. Something terrible is going to happen?"

Alasdair furrowed his brow. "Well, yes. But no one's said to have heard the Cù-Sìth bark for more than twenty years."

Blair felt a sly smile creeping across her face. "Of course, you don't believe any of this."

Alasdair cleared his throat, not quite meeting her gaze. "To be honest, a kelpie is seeming less and less unlikely by the minute."

Blair treated that as a private victory, but she didn't want to let on to Alasdair. She put her hands on her hips and looked out across the island, noting where the deer were clustered: in the meadows, along the ridges.

"The deer don't hang out in bogs much, do they?"

Alasdair shook his head. "They go where the good grazing is."

Blair chewed the inside of her cheek for a moment. "Let's say I knew that the kelpie was preying on deer."

Alasdair frowned at her, but he was already irresistibly following her line of reasoning. "Then bogs wouldn't be the most likely location," he admitted. "And we've ruled out the burns."

Blair squinted into the distance. A thick silver line wound down from the hills towards the village. "What's the river called?"

Alasdair followed her line of sight. "The Irving."

"Do the deer come close to it?"

Realisation was dawning across his face. "Yeah. There's good grazing in the floodplains … And there's one place in particular they like to go to drink."

The next day, Blair left her bike resting outside the Sea Stag Inn and wandered towards the bridge, walking in the middle of the empty road. A thick fog hung over the island once again, shrouding the village so completely that she could barely see ten metres ahead of her. It was less than ideal weather for kelpie hunting, but Blair couldn't bear the thought of waiting around at home when she could be making progress.

She was wearing her mum's boots again, and an old anorak of her dad's that she'd found. Although the boots were on the larger side and the waterproof had a certain wet-dog smell to it, Blair couldn't deny feeling a sense of pride that she was learning how to prepare for the weather.

Alasdair had let her borrow his map overnight, which she considered a pretty big honour. She studied it as she made her way over to their agreed meeting place. The bridge crossed the mouth of the River Irving, and they'd made a plan to follow the footpath that led from the sea to the pool where the deer came to drink.

Blair lowered the map and saw a shape emerging from the fog ahead of her. Alasdair was already waiting, but he wasn't alone.

The person standing beside Alasdair looked very much *like* Alasdair, but was about half his height. He had a mop of untidy sandy hair, and wore a T-shirt with a picture of a puffin beneath a bright yellow raincoat.

"Hello." Blair stopped before them. "Who's this?"

"My brother." Alasdair sounded a bit sheepish. "I have to babysit him today. Mum and Dad are both working."

Blair looked down at the mini-Alasdair. "Hi. I'm Blair."

His hand was pressed over his mouth, but through his fingers he replied, "I'm Ewan."

Blair gave Alasdair a meaningful look. "He's tiny! He looks like the perfect snack for a kelpie. We can't take him with us!"

Alasdair glanced sidelong at his brother, but Ewan was distracted by a rabbit in the grass. "I can't very well leave him alone, can I?" he whispered.

Blair sighed. "We're going to have to be extra careful."

"It won't make a difference, since a kelpie is a *mythical creature*," Alasdair shot back.

Blair opened her mouth to retort and then thought better of it. He had seemed pretty well convinced yesterday, but when he was in this sort of mood it seemed pointless to remind him. "Let's go."

She peered over the edge of the bridge to the River Irving beneath. The water was clear in the shallows, pebbles gleaming on the riverbed. In the centre, where the river was deepest, it was sapphire blue. She walked around the bridge, onto a dirt path beaten into the riverbank by many pairs of feet over many years.

They left the village behind, climbing a gentle slope. With the river beside her and the path beneath her feet, Blair wasn't too worried about losing her way, although it was eerie to be so blinkered by the fog.

"It's called rouk," Alasdair said, reading her mind. "This

95

kind of sea mist. It rolls in overnight and burns off by the afternoon. It's a Scots word, but we adopted it."

"Rrrrrouk," Blair repeated, trying to roll the 'R' like Alasdair did. The word seemed appropriately spooky.

Their footpath dwindled to a narrow trail that Blair suspected was kept in use only by deer. Eventually the ground levelled out to a windswept plateau: browning grasses and black bog with verdant reeds springing from their banks.

The rouk seemed to muffle all the sound around them, like a blanket thrown over the landscape. Blair was startled when she heard small footsteps approaching.

"Mum says you're an incomer," Ewan said politely. Alasdair sucked his teeth in embarrassment.

"We're new here, but my parents have always wanted to live on Roscoe," Blair explained. "My dad's sort of Scottish anyway."

"How can you be *sort of* Scottish?"

"Well, his mum's Scottish, but his dad is Polish."

"So are you Polish too?"

"I'm from Carlisle, which is in Cumbria, in the north of England. Both of my parents grew up there too. So I'm Cumbrian, and maybe a bit Polish and a bit Scottish."

Ewan mulled this over for a few moments. "My dad's from overseas. And my mum's Roscoenean."

Blair chuckled. "Is that what you lot call yourselves?"

"No, that's Ewan's invention," Alasdair laughed. "Look, we're almost at the spot I was telling you about. See how the river's widening? In a minute we'll come to a big pool.

It's a very popular spot for the deer to come and drink. I've seen—"

He stopped speaking suddenly. Blair had been looking out at the river, but when she turned back to the path she saw a figure emerge from the fog ahead. She stopped dead.

There was an animal on the path, half-cloaked in mist. Its coat glistened in shades of auburn and umber. It was thicker and taller than the largest stag she'd seen on the island, with a longer face and stronger legs. A mane and tail black as the deepest loch drifted in the light breeze.

It was, unquestionably, a horse – but at the same time, there was something distinctly un-horselike about it. Perhaps it was the pond-green bridle on its head, reins dangling to the ground as though its rider had recently taken a tumble into the river. Perhaps it was the creature's eyes – shark-black and glassy, and fixed unwaveringly on the three humans standing opposite it.

"Oh dear," Alasdair said faintly.

"Whose horse is that?" Ewan asked.

"That's not a horse," Blair said in a low voice.

If it *had* been a horse, it would have looked away from them by now and started grazing, or even wandered away to eat in peace somewhere else.

This creature was still staring at them.

"It's a kelpie," Alasdair breathed.

If Blair hadn't felt fairly sure that her survival depended on keeping the kelpie in her sights, she would have given him a *very* smug look in that moment.

"What do we do?" Alasdair asked.

Blair zeroed in on the reins that trailed along the ground. "If we get hold of its reins, maybe we can control it. Then we can lead it away. Get it on the ferry or something…"

"That's a terrible plan," Alasdair hissed, but Blair shrugged his comment off.

"I'll figure that part out later. You two stay here."

Blair couldn't believe she was about to do this. The creature staring at her would eat her alive. She could see that in the intensity of its gaze, and it made her hands shake. But it was her ticket out of this whole mess – the only way she was going to get home.

Taking a deep breath, Blair started walking towards the horse. It didn't look away, didn't even seem to blink.

When she was barely a metre away, the kelpie moved suddenly and she flinched – but it was only turning sideways, presenting her with its back. Its coat looked soft and warm. When she was little she had been desperate to learn how to ride, but they'd never had the money.

If she wanted to, she could climb up and they could canter into the hills right now. She could live her childhood dream.

No. She had to remind herself that this *wasn't* a horse. She had a job to do.

She took a step towards the bridle, but the creature turned its head and – without touching her – nudged her towards its back. *It really wants me to mount,* Blair realised with wonder.

And why shouldn't she, really? If she was on the back of a kelpie, no one could stop her from galloping into the village and boarding the next ferry out of this place. She could ride all the way home to Carlisle.

No, Blair told herself firmly, again. *The moment I touch it, it'll drag me into the river and I'll be dead.*

Her heart thundered. She was so close now that she could hear the huff of its breath, smell the brackish scent of its fur. One wrong move and it could have her in its teeth. Blair clenched her fists, then flexed her fingers.

She grabbed for the reins.

The kelpie tossed its head high and Blair's hands slipped on the slimy bridle. She stumbled backwards a step as she lost her grip, and the kelpie was on her in a flash, spinning round to lash at her with its teeth.

Blair didn't feel the moment the bite connected with her, but she heard the tearing of fabric. She floundered backwards into something – Alasdair.

"Come on!" He grabbed her by the sleeve and they ran.

IRVING

They ran from the river and the path, into the shelter of a copse of wind-stunted pine trees. Behind them, the kelpie raised its head and let out a shrill, unearthly whinny.

The fog was beginning to lift, and from the trees Blair could still see as far as the river.

The kelpie was following. But the most frightening thing about its pursuit was that it didn't appear to be in any hurry. While Blair, Alasdair and Ewan caught their breath, the creature walked after them slowly.

Blair guided Ewan and Alasdair deeper into the pines. When she glanced back, she saw that the kelpie was gazing at the far side of the river, where a heron was creeping with long, orange legs in the shallows. The two creatures' movements flickered in and out of view as they passed behind the trees.

Then there was a screech and a splash. Blair clutched her chest and she saw Alasdair slap a hand over Ewan's eyes, but the boy's mouth was already hanging open.

A few moments later, heart thudding, Blair saw the kelpie emerging from the water, its fur dripping wet. There were grey-blue feathers at the corner of its mouth.

In unspoken agreement they moved deeper into the trees, until they could see nothing but fog on all sides.

"Horses don't eat birds!" Ewan shrieked, halfway between terror and excitement. Alasdair shushed him quickly.

Blair had never felt so much adrenaline coursing through her veins – not even at the first strike, when the police had pulled up and demanded to know what they were doing and why they weren't in school.

"I told you!" she whispered. "A kelpie. I found it."

"*We* found it," Alasdair corrected.

"You didn't even believe it was real. And now—"

"Now it's almost bitten your head off. Not to mention, torn your waterproof."

Blair felt for the rip in the front of her jacket, though she tried not to let Alasdair see that her hands were trembling. He wasn't wrong; a centimetre closer and the kelpie would have taken a chunk out of *her*.

"I've never been happier to see humans," said a new voice, close at hand.

All three of them jumped at the sound, already on edge. Blair spun around and found herself face to face with – a kid?

They leaned casually against a tree trunk, arms folded. On closer inspection, they didn't really seem to be a kid at all – they were short, with smooth, frost-blue skin and skinny limbs, but their grey eyes had that same ageless quality that Cailleach's had. They were dressed in some kind of heavy cerulean poncho that fell to their feet, and their hair was a thick silver halo.

"I've been trying to scare that thing off for days, but nothing works," they continued wearily, as though they were all old friends catching up.

When Blair had finished gaping like a fish, she squeaked out, "Who are you?"

"Irving," they sighed, then held up a hand as if to halt questions the others hadn't been asking. "Yes, *that* Irving. This is my river. And I haven't got so much as a toe wet in days thanks to that thing – it gives me the creeps. I'm drying out." They ran a hand down the skin of one bony arm and shuddered.

"Are you…" Blair racked her brain for the word Cailleach had used to describe herself – "a guardian? You protect the river?"

Irving laughed. "I *am* the river."

Blair supposed that was a yes. The thought made her uneasy, but Irving wasn't quite giving her the same vibes as Cailleach.

"A kelpie is the *last* thing I need right now," Irving went on. "I've been flat out every summer lately just trying to keep the water cool enough for the salmon. Do you have any idea how particular those guys can be?"

"Look," Alasdair said in a hoarse whisper. "You're the spirit of the river, that's fine, whatever. Can we get back to the matter at hand? Like the horse that wants to eat us all?!"

"It's not a horse," Ewan said.

"Okay, the kelpie!" Alasdair covered his face with one hand. "I can't believe I brought my little brother KELPIE HUNTING."

"Kelpie hunters!" Irving echoed excitedly. "Perfect! So, what's the plan?"

Blair looked from Alasdair to Irving and back again. Even Ewan was watching her expectantly now, so she needed to come up with something.

"It wasn't letting me anywhere near its head," she reasoned. "I think we need a distraction while I go in for the bridle. If I can just get hold of it..."

"...you'll trap it in its horse form. Yeah, I know how this works." Irving waved a hand impatiently.

"Yeah," Blair said, as though she'd known that all along. "Exactly?"

"Well, don't expect *me* to be the bait." Irving crossed their arms.

"I have to be the one who takes the bridle," Blair put in quickly. "It's a hunter thing. Now here's what we're going to do..."

When the plan had been settled and their roles agreed, they gathered at the edge of the woods. The fog was evaporating quickly now, and there were large patches of blue sky overhead. They could all clearly see the kelpie watching a couple of deer grazing further down the riverbank. For the time being, at least, it appeared to have forgotten them.

Blair gave Irving a gentle prod and the river spirit crept reluctantly forwards. The kelpie's eyes found them at once and it watched their approach with ferocious intensity.

While Irving took slow steps towards the creature, Blair crept along inside the treeline until she was behind it. She glanced back to make sure that Alasdair and Ewan were out of danger, well back in the trees. Alasdair gave her a terse nod.

When Irving reached the kelpie's head, it wheeled around and presented them with its back, just as it had with Blair.

"No, thank you…" Irving said warily. As Blair crept up behind, Irving made a sudden unplanned lunge for the bridle. The kelpie spun around, reared up and struck out with one of its front legs. Irving yelped and ducked out of the way.

Blair seized her chance when the kelpie landed on all fours again, but she wasn't even close when the creature wheeled around and fixed her with those predatory eyes. She froze.

Irving was back on their feet, and they jumped fearlessly towards the kelpie, stealing its attention away from Blair. Blair's breath was coming fast, but there was no time to lose. She gritted her teeth and dove towards its ears once more, but the second her hand brushed the bridle, the kelpie whipped around like lightning, surging towards her with its teeth.

Blair staggered backwards a step, trying to grasp a plan through the fear that clouded her mind. It wasn't working!

The thing was too fast for them…

"HEY!" yelled a voice close at hand. "OVER HERE!"

It was Alasdair! He had jumped out of the trees and set off running along the riverbank, cutting a fine line between the creature and the river. The kelpie was torn – with Irving on one side, Blair on the other, and Alasdair flying past, it didn't seem to know where to look. White crescents flashed at the edges of its eyes, its ears flattening against its neck.

This was Blair's moment. She leapt forwards again and managed to slip her fingers under the bridle and grab on. The kelpie let out a shrill, bone-chilling cry as it threw its head this way and that, and Blair's arm jarred in its socket as she was hurled from side to side.

With another shriek, the kelpie dragged its head down, then tossed it upwards so quickly that Blair was thrown back by the sheer momentum of it. Her heels lost their purchase on the bank and for a moment she was weightless – the air seemed to crackle – then water came crashing over her.

"BLAIR!"

The shout was the only thing she heard as she broke the surface of the river, gasping. Alasdair was at the bank already, reaching down to pull her out.

She was soaked, and shocked, but the water was only waist-deep. When Blair reached out to clasp Alasdair's hand she found that she was already holding something.

It was the bridle. It was the colour and texture of

seaweed, tough as leather, and damp. But it was out of focus. Blair touched her nose and found her glasses missing. She plunged her hands into the water and felt around her feet, and after a moment, miraculously, she felt the frames wedged in between the pebbles.

"Where's the kelpie?" she asked urgently as she shoved her glasses back onto her face. Alasdair helped her up onto the bank, and there was no need for an answer because she saw it at once, even through the droplets that distorted her lenses.

The creature was rearing and bucking, spinning and kicking, alternating between squeals and a snort so drawn-out and pained it was almost a roar. Finally, it threw all its weight into its back legs, pawing at the air, and there was a burst of violet light so bright that all of them were forced to turn away.

When Blair looked back again, blinking away the halo from the flash, the horse was still there. It was panting where it stood, nostrils flaring.

"I think we did it," Irving said breathlessly.

Blair held tightly to the dripping bridle in her hand. Cailleach's voice echoed in her head: *A kelpie has been preying on my deer. Find it and do away with it.*

The animal lowered its head and snatched a few mouthfuls of grass, watching them as it chewed. Just a few minutes earlier, it hadn't shown the slightest interest in the grass beneath its hooves.

Ewan crept out of the trees. Alasdair held out a hand and guided his little brother behind him.

Blair took off her glasses and tried to dry them off, but her clothes were all soaked through. Noticing what she was doing, Alasdair reached out, and Blair let him take them. He pulled the hem of his T-shirt out from under his fleece and dried them with care. She smiled gratefully as she put them back on.

"I'm going to make sure," Blair said with more conviction than she felt. She approached the kelpie-horse, which was now guzzling grass as though it hadn't eaten in weeks. When she came close, it lifted its head high and snorted, but she held out her hands and made soothing noises until it settled again.

Tentatively, she laid a hand against its warm neck. It looked at her curiously, the predatory gleam in its eyes gone. Its irises had turned a rich, mundane brown.

Losing interest in her, the animal returned to grazing.

"We did it," Blair said, letting out a long sigh of relief. "I think it's trapped in horse form."

Irving laughed with glee and, without further ado, leapt into the river. A great spray of water went up, and then they resurfaced, giggling, and dove under again.

Their joy was infectious. Since Blair was already wet through, there was no harm in joining them. She jumped into the water and landed on her feet. Her heart was still racing in her chest, and she took a moment to breathe deeply and let it slow as the river rushed around her waist.

Irving spat a stream of water at her and Blair splashed them back. In response, Irving sent a shoal of bright silver-orange fish darting around Blair's legs, which startled Blair so much she fell over.

As Blair floated on her back, she couldn't help but grin. Here she was, splashing about with a river spirit after taking on a murderous shapeshifter. She could hardly believe it.

"Don't you want to come in?" she called to Alasdair. He was helping Ewan take off his shoes and roll up his trousers, but he shook his head.

"I don't swim."

Ewan waded in up to his knees and Alasdair sat on the bank to watch as they played in the water.

Eventually, Blair drifted over to him. "Thank you," she said, meaning it.

Alasdair shrugged, a troubled tilt to his mouth.

The whole river seemed to light up, and warmth prickled across Blair's back and shoulders. She looked up at the sky; all that was left of the fog were wisps of white against a bright, cloudless blue.

Ewan gasped. Irving had summoned an animal Blair had never seen before, with a long, sinuous body that was bark-brown and sleek. An otter.

For a moment, Blair's wonder faltered. The otter and the fish responded to Irving the way the deer did to Cailleach, and remembering the other guardian made Blair's mouth go dry.

But that had been the whole point – she was doing this to get *home*.

So why did she feel like a cloud had passed over the sun again?

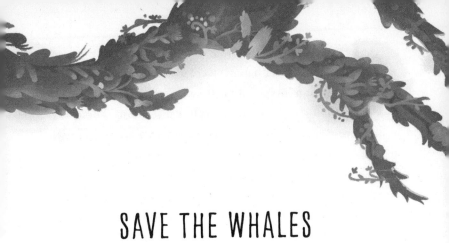

SAVE THE WHALES

Blair's parents had no idea that their daughter had a kelpie bridle hanging in her wardrobe. It was strange to think of her uncanny trophy hanging behind the closed doors of the new flatpack wardrobe, in amongst her clothes. It was the morning after their misadventure, and Blair could hear her mum and dad talking in the kitchen. For a moment it seemed impossible that her parents' plans and Cailleach's tasks existed in the same world.

Yawning, Blair put on her glasses, rolled out of bed and pushed open the window. The baby bird was still tucked up in its nest, but at the noise overhead it stretched out its wings and chirped up at her.

They really were wings now. It was amazing how fast the little creature seemed to be growing. Blair gazed at its big, round eyes and the hooked beak in the centre of its heart-shaped face. She suspected that it was some kind of owl.

At the breakfast table, Blair hastily gulped down her

morning cereal. Her parents were quietly drinking mugs of black coffee; a long to-do list lay ominously in the centre of the table, a few items already scored out. There was a hand-drawn calendar at the bottom of the page, with boxes crossed through for each passing day. In the final box, in bold letters, was written ROSCOE NEEDS YOU INSPECTION!

Her mum and dad seemed too tired to even quiz her about her plans, so as soon as Blair had finished eating she set off across the machair, her boots dry again, the bridle stuffed into her backpack.

Wagtails and swifts zoomed low over the meadow, while long-legged sandpipers paced between the stalks. She'd started borrowing her dad's wildlife guidebooks when she went out sketching, so she could at least label her drawings correctly. The air hummed with the flight of insects, and a pollen-drunk bumblebee drifted lazily past Blair's ear.

When Blair reached the standing stone at the summit of the hill, she was surprised to find that she still had enough breath to fill her lungs and call, "Cailleach?"

Her heart fluttered in her chest as she waited for an answer. A small part of her still wondered if that first encounter had been a dream, but the weight of the antler bracelet around her wrist told her differently, and there had been nothing uncertain about the adventure she'd had the day before.

"You've dealt with the kelpie?"

Blair spun around to find Cailleach only a few steps away from her. Somehow she was even taller than Blair remembered, and that wasn't counting the antlers, which seemed to tower into the sky. Blair nodded mutely.

"And I'm to take your word for it?" Cailleach said archly.

Blair couldn't ignore the way her heart sank. Compared with Irving, Cailleach was just so… intimidating.

Shrugging out of the backpack, Blair tugged the zip open, lifted out the riverweed bridle and held it up for the guardian to examine. "Is that enough proof?"

Cailleach's thick eyebrows lifted a fraction. "Well, well. I am impressed. One less predator for my deer to worry about."

Blair couldn't help but remember what Alasdair had said about the deer population – wasn't the Biodiversity Trust talking about introducing large predators to the island? Cailleach wouldn't be happy about that…

Blair stuffed the bridle back into her bag, since Cailleach didn't seem to want it. She had to stay focused. She needed to get home to Carlisle and Libby, and there was no time to waste.

"That's one task done, then," she said, trying to make herself sound casual and capable all at once. "What's next?"

Cailleach clucked her tongue. "Such a hurry. Still, there is another issue that might benefit from a human touch."

She folded her arms across her chest, looking out towards the village. "Roscoe emerged from the seas millions of years ago, but the island will always have water running through its veins. Everything is blurred here, constantly shifting: land and sea, earth and fey, human and seal…"

Blair found herself getting caught up in the guardian's words, but it was hard to parse the true meaning from them. There was no doubt that every word she said would turn out to be important, but what exactly was she asking Blair to do?

Cailleach was looking at her sidelong, and her eyes narrowed ever so slightly. A butterfly floated past, and Cailleach reached out a hand towards it. The butterfly alighted on her fingers.

"Some beings can change their form as freely as water changing its course. But a creature can be trapped, just as a river can be dammed."

Blair thought of the kelpie's eyes shifting from glossy black to brown, its manner altered from predator to prey. How lost it had looked when they'd headed home the day before: alone on the moor, startling at every noise. It had followed them for a little while, then drifted off on its own.

Cailleach closed her hand around the butterfly, and when she unfurled her fingers again, it was gone. In its place was a small, shiny red bead: a ladybird.

"Find the selkie that is unknowingly being held captive on this island. Set it free. That is your second task," she declared. The ladybird unfurled its black wings and lifted off from her hand.

"Selkie," Blair murmured, testing the word. The ladybird sailed past her face and she followed its flight, its whole life changed. In a moment it had disappeared from sight, and when Blair opened her mouth to ask her first question, Cailleach too was gone.

Blair hung the bridle up in her wardrobe again, deep in thought about what to do next. Cailleach had been characteristically unhelpful, but Blair didn't feel quite as lost as she had the last time. From the guardian's description it had sounded like selkies were shapeshifters too, and she'd said something that had stuck out to Blair – about the boundaries blurring between *human and seal*… That had been unusually specific.

"Blair!" her mum called, and a moment later the door to her room banged open. "Blair, I'm calling you!"

"You barely gave me a second to reply!" Blair said, whirling around.

Ignoring her, her mum asked, "You at a loose end today?"

Blair felt a flash of panic that she was about to be asked to help with the renovations. "I'm never at a loose end. I'm extremely busy. Well, if I had my *phone* and the *internet* maybe I would be—"

"Good. You said you'd visit Morag's mother and do a craft-afternoon with her, remember?"

"Crafternoon," Blair corrected, then immediately regretted it. "Mum, I *am* actually busy—"

But her mum interrupted. "I don't think it'd do you any harm to make some friends, instead of wandering the hills all day on your own."

"I already have a friend – well, sort of. That's who I've been wandering the hills with, and he's *my* age, and the fact that you think I'm desperate enough to befriend an old woman is actually offensive, besides which that generation has a lot to answer for in terms of their carbon footprints—"

Her mum held up a hand. "We're not getting into this again. You know how I feel about blaming entire generations, so stop trying to distract me. You made a friend?"

Her whole face had lit up. Blair felt herself shrinking away from it.

"Well, I guess so. I was thinking about going to see him this afternoon."

"Him?" She made an amused face.

"Mum, first of all, you can't just assume that everyone is straight – that's called being heteronormative. Secondly, obviously a boy and a girl can be friends. Thirdly, don't you think I have more important things to worry about than—"

"All right, I know. I'm sorry. Does your friend have a name?"

"Alasdair Reid."

Her mum's eyebrows shot up. "I suppose his mum is Aileen Reid, then?"

"Yep. Why?" Blair asked, but she could venture a guess.

"She's on the committee. Please go and visit Morag's mum. At the very least, maybe you can learn to make art for fun, not just to save the whales."

Blair couldn't stop herself. "The campaign to save the whales was one of the most successful environmental movements of the twentieth century!"

Her mum closed the door.

Blair found herself knocking on the door of the Fraoch Guest House after lunch. Despite what she'd said to her mum, she was actually intrigued by the old woman with the flinty eyes in the attic full of crafts.

"Blair Zielinski!" Morag answered the door. "You must be here for a crafternoon! Well, Mother'll be delighted. Maybe phone ahead next time, though. Sometimes she goes walking for hours on end. Anyway, you know where to go – you'll have to show yourself up!"

Blair was ushered to the staircase before she'd even got a word in. She ascended the stairs with a longing look at the computer alcove, then crossed the narrow hallway to the door.

"Back again, are you, spy?" came Rosemary's voice from within.

Blair pushed the door open. The old woman was hunched over her worktable, upon which was a bowl full of glass shards, a bottle of glue, a board on which pieces of glass had already been artfully arranged, and a ceramic pot. Blair was startled to realise that Rosemary had a hammer in her hand. She covered the pot with a cloth and brought the hammer down with a *smash*.

"Are you making a mosaic?" Blair asked.

Rosemary lifted the cloth to reveal the fragments beneath. "Aye," she said. "Crafternoon, is it? She's always

115

loved that term, my Morag." She chuckled, and her gaze, when it fell on Blair, wasn't so sharp after all.

Rosemary selected a piece of glass from the bowl and handed it to Blair. "Put some glue on the back of that, would you?"

Blair held up the glass, noticing how smooth its edges were, how it wasn't clear any more but an opaque, faded green. "Where did you get this?"

From the edge of her vision she saw Rosemary's eyebrows rise. "The beach." She sounded surprised. "Haven't you seen sea glass before? These shards have been rolled around on the ocean floor for longer than I could say. Then the sea spits them back out onto our shores."

Blair shook her head in wonder. "It's beautiful."

She reached for the glue and dabbed a little on the back, then handed the piece to Rosemary. The old woman positioned it carefully in the image. It seemed to depict an underwater scene; it reminded Blair of dappled light shining into water, seen from deep beneath the surface. Rosemary passed another shard to Blair, and on they went.

"I went out for a lovely walk yesterday morning," Rosemary said. "I love to be out in the rouk. So atmospheric."

"Oh yeah?" Blair replied, only half-listening as she worked.

"Indeed. I must look ancient to you, I suppose – and you're right, I am – but I still love a good ramble in the hills as much as I did when I was young."

116

"I'm sure."

"I walked up the river, along the western bank," Rosemary went on.

Blair paused momentarily, her heart picking up speed, but she made herself carry on as though everything was fine. "Really?" she said carefully. "You must have seen me. I was out with Alasdair and Ewan Reid, on the other side of the river."

"Well, hard to know what you're seeing in mist like that," Rosemary said, betraying nothing. "Did you three have a good time?"

"Yeah," Blair said, trying for nonchalance. "Just out for a walk. Ewan's very sweet. Alasdair can be a bit prickly, though. I'm not exactly sure if we're friends." She didn't quite know where this confession came from, but perhaps it would change the line of questioning.

"Hmm," said Rosemary contemplatively. "Alasdair Reid's been through a lot of changes in the past few years. I wouldn't be surprised if he has his guard up, but don't worry. He's a good lad. He's one of the most valuable members we have on the board of the Biodiversity Trust – full of energy and good ideas."

Blair blinked. "You're part of the Trust, too?"

Rosemary glanced at Blair's right wrist, or perhaps she was just looking at the piece of ceramic Blair had in her hand.

"Aye, lass," the old woman said. "You could make far worse friends on this island than Alasdair Reid."

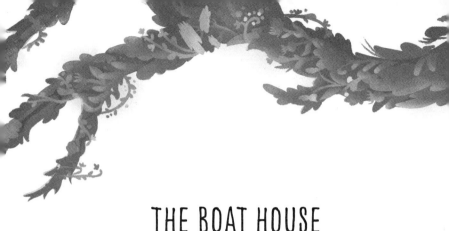

THE BOAT HOUSE

The following morning, Blair left her bike by the front gate of Alasdair's house and knocked on the front door, half-hoping no one was home. A seagull with a black head and black-tipped wings that looked like inky fingers cawed down at her from the roof.

Blair chewed her lip as she waited for someone to come, but to her relief it wasn't Aileen. The man who answered had the same sandy hair as his sons, though he was broader than Alasdair, with a heavier brow.

"Hello there," he said, his voice warm. "You must be Alasdair's new friend. I don't think we've met."

He held out his hand for her to shake, which took her by surprise given how the other adults of Roscoe had greeted her so far.

"Hi. I'm Blair."

"Sean. Come on in, he's just getting ready for the survey." He gestured her into the narrow hallway. The interior of the house had low ceilings, walls cluttered with photographs, and wooden toys and stuffed animals scattered all over the floor.

"Blair!" said a small, familiar voice, and Ewan came running over. He threw his arms around her legs and she smiled broadly.

"Hello, Ewan."

"I told Dad how we caught a kelpie." Ewan beamed up at her.

"Yes, I've heard *all* about it." Sean winked at Blair.

Phew. He had no idea.

"Want to show her up to your room?" Sean asked his son. "Alasdair's upstairs."

Ewan ran off, and Blair followed him up the winding stairs and into one of the bedrooms. One half of the room was littered with toys and clothes; the other was wallpapered with printed photos and pages ripped from magazines depicting everything from badgers to birds of prey, and of course, deer.

There were a few maps squeezed in amongst the wildlife. One was a map of the whole of Scotland, but it must have been from a long time ago as the paper was tea-coloured and fraying. There was Roscoe, a speck on the far west of the map, out past the Hebrides and deep into the Atlantic Ocean. There were multiple maps of the island too, some of them drawn by hand.

One map in particular was covered with cut-out pictures of animals: deer all over the hills, goats along the north of the island, dolphins out to sea, and along the coast, in an area marked *Whalebone Bay*, seals.

Alasdair stood in the middle of it all.

"What are you doing here?" he asked. He was fully dressed, but for some reason his face turned red. He quickly pulled a baggy hoodie over his T-shirt.

"Looking for you," Blair said, moving aside a stuffed toy fox to perch on the edge of Ewan's bed. "I've got another kelpie situation. Well, not a kelpie – a selkie. I don't know exactly. I wondered if you might want to help."

Alasdair, hands tucked into the pockets of his hoodie, hadn't moved from where he was standing. He looked at the floor between them, jaw working.

"I don't think so," he said stonily. "I'm sorry."

"Oh." Blair was taken aback. "Right."

Alasdair shifted uncomfortably. "It's just that… you shouldn't have let me bring Ewan. It was so dangerous! I can't put him at risk like that again."

Blair's mouth fell open. "That isn't fair! I *told* you not to bring him. You should have just stayed home!"

He was looking at her now, lips pursed. "It doesn't matter. I'm not helping you any more."

Seemingly oblivious, Ewan picked up the fox toy from the bed beside Blair and held it up to her. "This one is Mum's."

Blair tried to smile and gently pushed the toy away so she could stand up. Without a word, she turned and walked out of the room.

Ewan caught up to her as she reached the bottom of the stairs. "I can play the selkie game with you if you want."

Blair stopped in her tracks. "The selkie game?"

He nodded brightly. "We play selkies at school."

Blair glanced up at the bedroom doorway. If Alasdair didn't want to help her, fine. It didn't change anything. "Can you show me?"

Ewan grinned so widely she could see all his teeth. Before Blair could even ask the rules, he was tugging her out into the garden by the hand. "The grass is the sea. By the door is the land. I'm it, You RUN!"

He leapt towards her and a laugh escaped Blair as she zipped away from him.

"What happens if you catch me?" she called, but he was concentrating too hard to respond. Blair checked her stride and moved into his path. The little boy almost fell over in his enthusiasm to grab her sleeve.

"Got your skin!"

"What do I do now?"

"Now you're stuck on land." He pushed her towards the patio. "You've got to play too or it isn't fun," he said, and Blair realised that Alasdair was hovering in the doorway. Alasdair chewed his lip and then, without looking at Blair, he set off zig-zagging around the garden.

Ewan darted after him, but Alasdair wasn't playing along and it wasn't long before Ewan started to slow, his lips puckering in frustration.

"Alasdair!" Blair called in warning.

He looked over his shoulder, sighed, then pretended to trip and fell dramatically to the ground.

Ewan leapt on top of him. "GOT YOUR SKIN! Go to land!"

Alasdair made a show of walking with heavy steps to the house. Ewan followed him, practically skipping.

"I guess you win. You've got our skins," Blair said.

"No." Ewan shook his head primly. "You've got to get them back."

He took off running with a squeal. Alasdair leapt after him, and Blair gave chase as well. They ran with exaggerated slow moon-leaps as Ewan giggled and whizzed around them, until finally Alasdair caught him by one arm. Blair grabbed the other, triumphant.

"There you go. We got our skins back."

Blair noticed that someone else was now leaning in the doorframe, watching them play. It was Sean, a troubled set to his brow.

"Enough for now," he called out. "Ewan, there's a sandwich for you on the table."

Ewan's eyes lit up and he ran into the house without a backwards glance. Sean closed the door behind them, and Blair and Alasdair were left alone on the lawn.

Still panting, Blair sat down cross-legged on the grass. To her relief, Alasdair sank down beside her.

"So, selkies, huh?" he said.

Blair just glared at him.

"Okay, I'm sorry," he said. "I got spooked the other day. The kelpie, I mean – it was real! An actual killer shapeshifter, and we took it on. I shouldn't have brought Ewan. It was my bad decision, and I'm sorry I blamed you. But I want to keep him out of all this from now on."

"From now on?" Blair repeated uncertainly.

Alasdair smiled sheepishly at her. "Whatever this is, whatever you're doing... It's mad, but I want to help. How did you know there was a kelpie in the first place?"

"Someone asked me to look for it," Blair began. "I can't tell you who, so you'll just have to trust me. They asked me to look for a selkie as well. A trapped selkie."

Alasdair didn't question her any further; apparently he'd decided he would trust her. "There was a song about selkies on my granddad's cassette tape. I don't remember very well because someone recorded over it. Probably Ewan."

"All I know is something about the boundaries blurring between human and seal."

"Right. More shapeshifters. In the game, when you're a selkie, you're in the sea – that must be the seal part – but if someone gets your skin, you have to go to land."

"So it must be the *seal*skin. If you take a selkie's sealskin, they'll be trapped in human form, on land. Like taking the kelpie's bridle and leaving it stuck as a horse."

Alasdair was nodding now; Blair could practically see the cogs turning in his brain. She felt so relieved that he'd changed his mind – all of this was much more fun when he was on board. "This is starting to sound familiar. There's an old story about beautiful women leaving their sealskins on the beach, and men stealing them so the selkies had to marry them..."

"Ick," said Blair.

"I know. But how do we figure out which of the islanders is a selkie that's been trapped? There must be some kind of clue. I don't know anyone with whiskers..."

"What about those black shark eyes, like the kelpie had?"

Alasdair gave it some thought for a moment, but then he shook his head. "No. I can safely say I have never seen a person with black eyes on this island, and I *do* know everyone. I'm not joking."

"I know. You never joke." Blair caught his eye and he actually smiled. She lay back on the grass, staring up at the cloudless blue sky. What would it feel like to be trapped, far from home? Well, she could empathise, obviously. But who knew how long the selkie had been stuck in human form? What if it had been years – decades – since they'd seen their family?

Suddenly, she thought of her dad, who had grown up a long way from the place where he'd been born. His parents had spent half their lives in one country and half in another. Yet even now her dad drank his herbata, kept his jars of juniper and lovage and gherkins close at hand. It was a way of staying close to his first home, even though he was far away.

"I have a theory," Blair said, bolting upright. "If you were trapped on land, missing the sea, maybe you'd want to surround yourself with things that remind you of home – as a way to keep the sea close."

Alasdair drummed his fingers on his chin. He nodded slowly. "Yeah. That makes sense. At the very least, it's somewhere to start."

They spent the morning meandering through the village, but as they wandered up and down the streets Blair's spirits sank and her frustration rose. It seemed like *everybody* on Roscoe wanted to demonstrate their love of the Atlantic. There was barely a house or front garden that didn't have some marine knick-knacks on display: a collection of seashells here, a life ring there. At one house, yachting ropes and buoys were hung in a tree like fairy lights.

A slender white bird with a black head and a sharp red beak perched on the top of the tree and stared down at them. When they moved on, it soared and hopped along the rooftops, keeping pace with them.

"What's up with that bird?" Blair muttered to Alasdair.

He glanced up at it. "Arctic tern."

"It's following us."

Alasdair raised his eyebrows. "Seriously, Blair?"

"Remember what happened the last time you doubted me?"

He couldn't argue with that. They both kept an eye on the tern from then on as they moved through the village. Gradually, it was joined by a puffin and a guillemot, which Alasdair identified and declared "very weird".

All three birds watched the two of them with unnatural focus until finally Blair ran at the wall they had perched on and they scattered, flapping off in different directions.

They made their way past the row of B&Bs. Fraoch was closest, and the calico cat was prowling along the gutter at the edge of the roof. It paused to stretch its long body, and Blair found herself coming to a stop.

"I didn't notice this before," she said. She'd probably been too distracted by the tartan explosion inside the guest house. But now that she was looking at the exterior properly, she saw that there was a rowing boat near to the front door which had been turned into a garden bed, overflowing with flowers and shrubs. The boat was decorated with seashells and cuttlefish bones and dried-up starfish. Someone had spent a lot of time and energy on this.

"Looks a little suspicious," Blair said, glancing at Alasdair sidelong.

"It's just a coincidence," he replied as he surveyed the nautical garden. "Morag's husband left for the mainland years ago. Surely if she were waiting to return to the sea, she would have gone by now."

The front door opened, startling them both. Morag appeared, eyes narrowed in suspicion.

"What do we have here? Blair? Alice? Sorry – Alasdair!" Her face immediately reddened. "Something interesting about my flower beds?" she added hurriedly.

"We just hadn't noticed them before, Morag," Alasdair replied, not batting an eyelid. "Sorry for loitering. We'll be on our way."

They walked off, and Blair heard the door close only a moment later. She glanced back at the B&B.

"Why'd she call you Alice?" she asked. Alasdair hadn't seemed surprised by it in the slightest.

He shrugged. "It used to be my name. Some folk are still getting used to it."

Blair pushed her glasses up her nose as she digested this new information. Alasdair was checking his watch.

"I'll have to head home soon. I can't come tomorrow either. I'm a bit behind on the survey, I need to catch up."

"That's all right. I'll search on my own for a bit."

As they reached the gate to his house, Alasdair smacked his forehead. "I forgot! I've got to babysit Ewan tomorrow. And I'm not taking him with me into the hills – not after the other day."

"I could do that," Blair said. "Babysit, I mean. So you can do your survey."

Alasdair held her gaze uncertainly. "Really? What about finding your selkie?"

He made a good point. But somehow it felt slightly less urgent than it had before. "It can wait a day."

Alasdair's face broke into a smile so bright Blair felt a tug in her chest. "Thank you!" he said, and before she knew it he had wrapped her up in a hug. She laughed and pushed him off.

"Honestly, it's just keeping a small person alive. How hard can it be?"

"From one 'til four, if you can."

"I definitely can."

Her gaze slid past him to the house beyond, and in the light of their day's search, the building suddenly seemed to come into focus.

It had been a boat once; she'd known that for a while, of course. But it had been a *boat*. A vessel that lived its life on the waves. The path to the front door was lined with shells and there were sea-glass chimes hanging in the porch. The garden was full of strange plants like thrift and sea kale that she'd looked up in her dad's guidebooks when she'd been sketching on the shore – not like the ordinary roses and lavender that everyone else had. Even the higgledy-piggledy fence around the garden was made of driftwood and yachting rope.

"Alasdair—" she began, then stopped herself.

"What?" he asked, an easy smile on his face.

She couldn't say it. Not after everything they'd been through already, not when they finally seemed to be getting on. She glanced from the house to her friend and swallowed. "Nothing."

THE TREASURE HUNT

Though it was already half past noon when Blair left the house the next day, the world was still shrouded in mist. Blair stood at the front door looking out at the sea, its grey waters fading into the fog. There was something moving in the waves. Could it be the fairy cattle – the crodh mara?

She wheeled her bike down to the garden gate and let herself through. The shape in the water grew bigger as it moved from the depths into the shallows. The pale orb of the sun glowed behind the clouds, and Blair realised the creature was her mother.

The sea parted around her mum's ankles as she waded to shore. She picked up a towel and dried off her face, then wrapped it around her hair and squeezed.

Blair had so rarely seen her mum do anything other than rush. Hurrying out to work, coming home and going straight into the kitchen, passing her on the stairs carrying a laundry basket. Blair couldn't remember ever seeing her do something alone, something that couldn't be checked off a list or bring in a bit more money.

This moment of quiet belonged to her mother alone. Blair felt like she was trespassing.

"You're not coming in, then?" her mum said, noticing Blair. A small smile crossed her lips.

"I have to go into the village," Blair answered, so caught off guard she forgot to be sarcastic.

"You're very busy these days."

"I thought you'd be happy about that."

"Who said I wasn't?"

The front door banged closed behind them, shattering the moment. Blair's dad strode down the garden path and hopped over the wall, bypassing the gate Blair was blocking. He had a notebook in one hand and a pen in the other, and he stopped between them and said emphatically, "If you have any love for me at all, you will help me in my hour of need."

Blair's mum couldn't quite hide her smile. "Still stuck on a name?"

Blair looked between her parents, totally lost.

"Not just *a* name, kochanie. This won't just be the name of our business – it's the name of our *home*. It has to be… right. It has to be the *true* name of this place."

Blair took a moment to catch up. "You still haven't named the B&B?"

Blair's mum wrapped the towel around herself and folded her arms over her chest. "Your dad is a perfectionist."

"I'm going to be late." Blair started to wheel her bike forwards.

"Not so fast." Her dad clapped a hand on her shoulder. "I've got enough to think about already. I'm delegating. Blair, it's now your job to name our home."

Blair straightened up in surprise at this suggestion. But she needed to think quickly so she could get going. "Why don't you just call it—"

"Uh-uh!" Her dad pressed a finger over her lips to silence her. "Take some time and think about it. Remember what I said. It has to be perfect."

"No pressure then," Blair tried to say, but it came out muffled.

"Really, Józef?" Her mum sounded unconvinced, but her dad dropped his finger and turned around.

"I think Blair is the perfect person to figure out the true name of this place. Now, she's going to be late for babysitting. Blair, don't you think you'd better get going?"

Blair rolled her eyes, hopped onto the bike and started to pedal. She put the conversation out of her mind at once, ignoring the complicated feelings in her chest.

The house didn't need a name, because she wasn't planning on staying.

There was a black-headed gull sitting happily on the chimney stack when Blair reached the boat house. Sean answered the door when she rang. Was it her imagination, or was there something wary in his gaze? Then again, she felt quite uneasy about seeing him too, in light of her suspicions.

"Alasdair's already gone out," he said, opening the door wide to let her in. "Thanks for looking after Ewan. I've got the afternoon shift at the shop. I should be there already, really."

Ewan popped up over the back of the sofa, still in his pyjamas. "Blair!" He ran over to hug her leg.

"Hello Ewan," Blair said. "It's not a problem. We'll have fun, won't we?" She prodded Ewan's shoulder and he giggled.

"There's food in the fridge. Don't let him watch too much TV if you can help it. He has a tape he likes to listen to." Sean's keys were already jingling in his hand. "See you two later."

The door closed behind him.

Blair cleared her throat. "Want something to eat?"

Ewan nodded enthusiastically.

In the galley kitchen, Blair whipped them up a meal using what was available and her limited skills. They sat down at the table to a plate of noodle sandwiches – a speciality of Blair's, involving two slices of white bread and a packet of instant noodles.

"Someone forgot their phone." Blair pointed to a black slab on the table.

"It's for emergencies," Ewan answered with his mouth full.

Blair dusted off her fingers and picked it up, her heart suddenly quickening. "I'd better check that it's working," she said as calmly as she could manage – but Ewan was humming a song, not even looking at her.

The phone screen lit up: no password, which made sense. The battery was in the red, but Blair opened a browser anyway and checked her messages.

They started flooding in at once. There were more than two hundred since she'd logged in last, and her eyes widened as she scrolled through them. There were photos of the papier mâché skeletons in progress, sketches for banners, even some cool animal masks that people had started making. Blair felt a stab of jealousy and misery. She should *be* there, at the centre of all of this – just like Libby, posing with a half-painted badger mask in the most recent photo.

"Can we play a game?" Ewan asked, startling Blair.

"Finish your food first," she said. But as she looked back at the phone, the screen went black in her hand. The battery was dead. Blair set it down with a thud and returned to her sandwich.

Just being here, thinking what she was thinking, felt like a betrayal of Alasdair. Unconsciously she reached for the antler bracelet, turning it around her wrist. She couldn't pass up this chance to search for clues.

She had no idea how she was going to do it without Ewan noticing. If she could just put something good on TV and give him some sugary food, maybe he'd be so distracted she'd be able to get to work.

The thought put a sour taste in her mouth. But her chest was still aching… Libby seemed so busy and happy in all the photos, like she didn't even care that Blair was gone.

Only two tasks stood between her and getting off this island for good.

And there was the selkie, after all. Someone was trapped against their will. If she was right, she might be able to set them free.

"Where's that tape your dad said you like?" Blair asked, wandering through the archway into the living room.

"On the sofa," Ewan answered.

Blair found the ancient cassette player half-hidden under a cushion. She had never used one before, but there was an obvious PLAY button. She pressed it and it stuck down, but the wheels in the middle of the tape began to turn. The music that emitted from it was tinny: a fiddle and an old man's gravelly voice.

"Thrice barks the Cù-Sìth
And leaps on a-hunting..."

So this was the tape of their grandfather's songs Alasdair had mentioned. But Blair's roving gaze had landed on a wooden pirate ship, discarded in the corner, and she was struck by an idea. She set down the tape player and brought the ship into the kitchen.

"Want to play pirates?"

Ewan stuffed the rest of his sandwich into his mouth and nodded vigorously.

Blair scouted the living room and came up with a stuffed toy eagle, a silk scarf, a roll of tape, a wooden spoon and a spatula. The eagle she taped to her shoulder and the scarf she fastened around Ewan's head, covering one eye. He giggled as she placed the spatula in his hand and tucked the wooden spoon through a belt loop on her jeans.

There was a colouring book and a box of crayons on the table, so she flipped to a blank page in the back of the book and smoothed it out in front of Ewan. With a blue crayon she sketched a rough outline of the shape of the house. She pushed the crayons towards him.

"Arrrrrr! Cap'n, where be the loot in yer ship?"

Ewan grinned and upended the box, selecting a red one for himself.

"X marks the spot," Blair prompted. Ewan stuck his tongue between his teeth and got to work.

When he was finished, Blair picked up the map and examined it closely. There were several Xs marked around the house: a map of the Reid family's treasures. It occurred to Blair that she might have made a very good thief – a thought that made her feel kind of miserable.

The first X was right there in the kitchen. Ewan pointed to a high cupboard above the sink, and Blair reached up to open it. Inside was a set of dusty blue-and-white china plates and bowls. Blair glanced down at Ewan.

"They're Grandma's," he said. "We only get them out at Christmas."

"That's great," Blair said levelly. "What's next?"

Ewan consulted the map, then led her into the living room. He knelt down in front of the cupboard under the TV and opened the doors, rummaging around for a moment in the dark before resurfacing with a jar full of change.

"Good work," Blair said half-heartedly, patting him on the back. She was beginning to doubt that this plan was going to get her anywhere at all. But there were still two Xs left on the map, so she followed Ewan upstairs.

On the landing, Ewan opened a door so quietly and reverently that she knew at once it must lead to his parents' room. On the dressing table was a pretty wooden jewellery box, filled with earrings and necklaces. Beside the box was a large, pearlescent pink conch shell. But there was nothing remotely resembling a seal's skin.

Blair felt a shiver of unease travel down her arms. It didn't feel right sneaking around the family's house like this, looking at their valuables.

Ewan was looking expectantly at her, so she ruffled his hair and said "Arrrr, so much plunder, Cap'n!"

He waved the map in front of her face and said, "We're not finished!"

There was one X left.

Travelling back through the living room, a strain of the tape player's distorted music in the background caught in Blair's mind.

> "Great Guardian Cailleach, protector of the deer,
> Shared not Bodach's hope; the people brought fear..."

Her steps faltered, but Ewan shouted "Yo ho ho!" and she realised he was already standing in the open back door.

When Blair caught up to him, Ewan pointed past the overflowing veggie patch to a tumbledown shed in the corner of the garden. The wooden panels looked rotten with damp, and moss was growing on the roof.

"There's treasure in there?" Blair asked sceptically.

"Sometimes I see a torch in there at night," Ewan said in a quiet voice. "From my room, when I'm supposed to be asleep. Someone goes creeping in to check on something. I think it's pirate gold."

That's very *interesting*, thought Blair.

"Let's capture the treasure, Cap'n," she said.

Ewan raised his spatula high overhead. "Avast!"

They raced across the grass, but as they rounded the veggie patch, a voice stopped them dead in their tracks.

"*What* are you doing?"

They turned in unison to find Aileen standing in the doorway, her bag and coat slung over one arm as though she had just got in.

"The treasure!" Ewan said. "We have to find—"

Blair squeezed his shoulder quickly. "We're playing pirates."

Aileen narrowed her eyes. "I mean what are *you* doing in *my* house?"

Blair looked from her to Ewan and back, her heart hammering. This woman had a serious problem with her. Was it just because she was an incomer? Did she really hate outsiders that much? "I'm the babysitter," she said, even though it was obvious.

"She's a PIRATE!" Ewan burst out.

Aileen stepped to the side, opening up the doorway. "I think you should go."

Blair was speechless. She was just so *mean*. And Blair was trying to help...

Aileen took the wooden spoon from Blair's hands as she passed. Blair peeled the stuffed bird from her shoulder and lay it on the kitchen table. There were still crayons everywhere, and the unwashed remains of noodle sandwiches. The living room was tipped upside down from their treasure hunt.

Blair flushed with embarrassment; she doubted she was going to be asked to babysit again. But she couldn't worry about that now – she needed to stay focused.

She had a much more important job to do.

FIND THE SELKIE,
SET IT FREE

Blair got on her bike and pretended to ride it away, but as soon as she was out of sight she dismounted and pushed it into the driveway at Fraoch, where she hoped it wouldn't be noticed. She followed a narrow footpath around the back of the houses and crept along until she reached the familiar driftwood fence.

Heart racing, she hopped over and hid at the back of the shed. When she peeked around, she couldn't see anyone moving through the kitchen windows, but there was flashing light from the living room beyond, as though they'd turned on the TV.

She slunk around to the shed door and tugged at the padlock. It was firmly shut, but perhaps there was a key hidden somewhere.

Blair began hunting around, lifting up plant pots and garden gnomes to peek underneath. She checked above the doorframe and below the doormat, but there was nothing to be found.

Slipping back around the side of the shed, she tried the window, but it was jammed shut. Blair leaned against the wall while she thought about what to do next – her heart was hammering and she needed a moment to catch her breath. The rotten wood of the wall bowed inwards where she leaned. Curious, she placed two hands on the wooden panel and pushed.

The panel gave way with a *crack*. When it toppled inwards, it left an opening just large enough for her to shuffle through sideways. Blair glanced around the corner of the shed towards the house – no one seemed to have heard her.

Inside the shed, the only light was a grey glow from the grimy window. A canopy of spiderwebs hung from the ceiling, and every inch of the floor space and shelving was filled with shed-junk: a lawnmower, bags of compost and bird seed, a paddling pool, a swingball pole.

Everything was sprinkled with a thin layer of dust, like snow, which revealed an indistinct set of footprints from the door to a stack of crates in the far corner. There were scrapes and handprints in the dust on the wooden crates, as though they were regularly handled.

Blair picked her way across the shed and heaved down the top crate – it was full of plastic plant pots and spiders angry at being disturbed. She set it down on top of the workbench beside her and reached for the next.

The second crate was much heavier, filled with containers of liquid fertiliser. Blair wedged it onto the ground in amongst the junk and caught her breath.

The third crate was full of terracotta plant pots, but when Blair lifted it by the rope handles, one of them snapped. She dropped the crate with a heavy thud, and half of its contents spilled out and smashed on the floor.

Blair held her breath, hands shaking, as she waited for someone to come running out and find her in the middle of the chaos.

But something caught her eye – a clean blue tarpaulin without a speck of dust on it, spread out over the contents of the final crate. Blair reached for it at once, ran her hands over its crinkly surface and pulled it away.

Beneath was a shapeless mass of what might have been fabric, though it was an otherworldly shade of silver that seemed to give off a faint glow in the shadowy space. Blair picked it up, but it almost slipped through her fingers: the surface was smooth and damp, like a freshly caught fish.

She had never felt anything like it.

This had to be the sealskin.

"You found the treasure!" said a small voice behind her.

Slowly, Blair turned around. Ewan stood peering through the hole she had made in the wall, his scarf-eyepatch still tied in place.

For a moment Blair was too stunned to speak. Then she pressed a finger to her lips, urging him to keep quiet. Her mind raced. If he had heard her, he probably wasn't the only one.

She gazed at the small boy in his unicorn T-shirt and bare, muddy feet. Alarm bells were ringing in her mind:

this felt wrong, wrong, wrong. Sure, Aileen wasn't the nicest person in the world – especially to Blair – but she was Ewan's *mum*. Was Blair really going to separate a child from his mother?

But then again… was it even her choice to make? Because if she was right, Aileen was being kept here against her will. She thought that her skin was lost, that she'd never be able to return to the sea. But Blair had it here in her hands, and Aileen deserved to know. Whatever choice Aileen made then would be her own.

Blair stepped carefully over the shards of broken terracotta. She knelt down beside Ewan and held out her offering.

"Ewan, I think your mum might be a selkie," she said gently. "Like in the game. I think this is her sealskin. If you give it to her, she'll be able to go home."

Ewan took the item from her, sagging slightly under its weight. He stared down at it with his mouth twisted in confusion.

"Mum's a… selkie?"

Blair led the way to the front door, because turning up at the back door when she'd just been dismissed seemed like it might cause more alarm than necessary. Ewan had the skin clutched against his body and there was a determined set to his mouth as he jogged after her. Blair took a deep breath and knocked.

The front door opened to reveal Alasdair, still in his

mud-encrusted hiking boots, camera slung around his neck. His face creased in confusion as he took in the sight of the two of them together. Blair's mouth went dry.

"Alasdair – I didn't know you were home—" she started to stutter, but Alasdair's eyes went wide as they landed on the item Ewan carried, and he pulled the door closed behind him.

"What is this?" His voice was strangely hollow.

"It's a sealskin." Blair glanced through the window behind him; there was movement in the living room. "You know that."

"Where did you find it?" he whispered.

"In the shed."

"*Our* shed?"

"Yes."

"Well, it's not ours."

Blair waited until he met her gaze. "I think it is."

Alasdair shook his head fervently. "My dad is not *holding my mum hostage!*"

"I'm not saying that – I don't know what the situation is!" Blair whispered in a hiss. "I just know that this skin was hidden in your shed. And if it is hers, shouldn't she have the right to choose between the land and the sea?"

"Why are you getting involved? Why is it so important to you to find this selkie? And the kelpie? What difference does it make to you?" Alasdair's voice was hoarse.

"It's my only chance to go *home*!" Blair shot back without thinking. "You wouldn't understand. I want to go home, that's all. And if I do these things, I'll be able to."

Alasdair stared at her for a moment. "You're doing all this to leave the island?"

Before Blair could answer, the front door swung open. Aileen grimaced at the sight of Blair. "I thought I told you to—"

But then she saw what Ewan held in his hands, and her face blanched.

Behind Blair, the gate squeaked as someone came into the garden. Aileen watched them approach but seemed unable to move.

"Everyone all right?" Sean asked, joining them all. "You look like you've seen a—"

But when he saw what Ewan was holding, he stopped speaking. Sean looked at Aileen and something charged and heavy passed between them. The gears clicked into place in Blair's mind.

She lifted the skin from Ewan's hands and held it out to Sean. He took it from her without a moment's hesitation, grasping it tightly against his chest.

"Don't go," Aileen said quickly.

Sean took a step back from her, his whole body guarded.

"Dad?" Alasdair said, like a lamb's frightened bleat.

Sean looked from Alasdair to Ewan and back again, his chest rising and falling heavily. His fingers were gripping the skin so tightly they'd turned white. "I'm so sorry," he choked out. "I can't." In the next breath, he was running.

Sean leapt the garden fence like a deer, sprinted across the road without checking for traffic and tore down the narrow lane between the shop and the pub. He reached the edge of the harbour, leapt into the air and dropped out of sight.

There was a huge splash, then silence.

For a heartbeat, no one moved. Then Alasdair knocked Blair aside as he ran after his dad. Blair gathered herself and followed him.

Ripples were spreading from the site of the impact, but otherwise the water was still. The skin didn't come floating up from the deep; Sean didn't resurface.

Blair's heart seemed to have stopped beating altogether. Her ears rang as she looked back over her shoulder at the house, to where Aileen stood in the doorway, Ewan clinging to her legs.

Alasdair's weight shifted as he turned away from the water, towards Blair. His eyes were full of tears.

"How could you do this?" The hurt in his voice made Blair's chest ache.

"Your— he's free now," Blair stammered, grasping for the reasons that had seemed so convincing only minutes earlier. "He can come and go. It'll be okay... It wasn't right—"

Alasdair covered his face with his hands, shaking his head. "You don't know anything!" he shouted. When he dropped his hands, his jaw was set. "I listened to the end of the seal song on my granddad's tape last night – the only part that wasn't taped over. I was doing research for *you*! Selkies who find their skins *never come back*, Blair. My dad is never coming back."

He started walking towards the house. Blair set off after

him, her mind buzzing so loudly she could barely think. There had to be a solution, a way she could fix this—

"Just leave me alone!" Alasdair yelled at her. "Leave my whole family alone. I'm glad you're leaving. You'd never have belonged here anyway."

WHERE THE FEY
HOLD SWAY

Most of the time, Blair was good at keeping her emotions below the surface. Letting her anxiety simmer was something she was used to, but it was all becoming too much.

Once, her life had been normal. She needed to remember that. She needed to get *back* to that.

Speeding down the road towards the house on her bike, she tried to remember if she'd ever felt this awful back in Carlisle. She didn't think so. She'd felt miserable, sure, when her parents had first found out she'd missed a day of school to protest – they'd been furious, they wouldn't even listen to her reasons, too caught up in the fact that she hadn't asked for permission.

She'd been scared when one of the older kids had shaken up a can of spray paint and scrawled DON'T LET OUR FUTURE BURN on the council building, and the police had surrounded them all and taken him away in the van. But it had only been chalk paint, and no one pressed charges. That had been at their last strike: the biggest one they'd organised yet. There had been thousands of kids in the streets, hand-painted signs bobbing over their heads like boats on a stormy sea, a chorus of chanting voices. The atmosphere had been electric. She'd never felt more like everything was going to be okay.

Now, she had no idea what was happening. She couldn't even keep up with the group chat. It had been weeks since she'd spoken to anyone.

And Libby. Her best friend. The one person who seemed to completely understand her anxieties, who cared just as much as she did about changing the world.

She needed to speak to Libby.

When she reached the house, Blair discarded her bike on the grass and let herself in through the front door as quietly as possible. She tiptoed upstairs, though one of the steps creaked unhelpfully under her weight.

She could hear her mum humming in one of the guest bedrooms, the whirring of paint rollers on the walls. The door was ajar but not closed; Blair crept past it, holding her breath, and stepped into her parents' bedroom. The curtains were drawn, the room dim.

Blair moved around to her dad's side of the bed and opened the drawer of his bedside table. Her phone was nestled in amongst the collection of crumpled papers, loose change and elastic bands, its screen dark and lifeless. She held down the power button, then pressed a fist to her mouth with silent joy when the screen lit up.

It took a moment to load, but when she finally unlocked

the screen she saw, with relief, a single bar in the corner. In the next moment the notifications came flooding in, her phone buzzing constantly in her hand. Red bubbles in the corners of her apps told her she'd missed dozens more messages in the planning chats, and there was a timeline of messages from Libby going back to the day they'd last spoken. The most recent read:

> guess you're done with us then?

Blair's heart leapt into her mouth. She looked further back.

> trying not to take this personally...

> hope you just don't have signal??

> seriously where are you

> B I need your thoughts on the design I shared!!

Blair's eyes filled with tears as she took in the scale of the damage, and she angrily dashed them away. How could Libby think that she would just move on the moment she left the mainland?

Blair took a deep breath and began to tap out a response. She typed, deleted and retyped her message, hurt but not wanting to begin in anger, unsure how to possibly summarise the events of the past weeks.

The sound of a throat clearing froze her thumbs. She looked up slowly.

Her dad was silhouetted in the doorway. His face was unreadable, but he beckoned with a jerk of his head for her to come out.

"Just let me finish this message, Tata," Blair said quietly, not wanting to draw her mum's attention.

"Put it down." His voice was equally low; he must have had the same idea.

"Please. Libby thinks I'm ghosting her."

He just shook his head. "You know you're not allowed."

Blair hovered with the phone clutched in her hands. Finally she moved to set it down.

"What's this?"

It was her mum's voice. Blair dropped the phone like a hot potato; it bounced on the mattress.

"You're not letting her use her phone?" Her mum looked at her dad in shock. He shook his head silently.

"I'm leaving!" Blair said, edging around the bed towards the door.

Her mum stepped into the doorway, blocking her exit.

"Did you break into our room to use your phone?"

"I didn't 'break in' – the door was open and this is my house too!" Blair shot back.

"You are *forbidden* from using that phone, Blair! You need a clean break. Can't you just make the most of what's right on your doorstep? Stop worrying about the strikes for a few weeks and just *live your life!*"

"This *is* about my life!" Blair spluttered. "This is about my future. My whole generation. I can't just shut my eyes and pretend nothing's happening, like – like you!"

Her mum folded her arms across her chest, her face stony. "You need time to settle in."

"I don't *want* to settle in! Why can't you respect that?"

"Respect!" Her mum snorted. "You don't know what that word means."

"Yes I do. And if you think I don't have it, it's because I don't respect *you*! We could have just moved to the countryside or something, stayed close. But you dragged me out to the middle of the ocean instead! You're literally stopping me from fighting for the most important thing in the world. You don't care about what's happening to the planet, you don't even pretend to! You're so selfish!"

Her voice rose with every sentence until she was practically yelling in their faces. Her dad looked away, his jaw tightening. Her mum held Blair's gaze, her chest rising and falling heavily.

"Why did it have to be Roscoe? Why here?" Blair went on, though she was beginning to doubt herself. "I wish you'd just left me behind!"

In the dim room, Blair's mum's face was cast in shadow. It was only when her mum turned and her cheeks caught the light from the hall that Blair realised there were tears streaming down her face.

Blair caught her breath, opened her mouth to say something. But her mum just walked back to the guest room without a word.

When her dad looked her way, she hoped to see some understanding on his face, one of their shared Mum's-being-a-bit-grumpy moments. There was nothing there but dismay. "Go to your room, Blair."

Blair did not go to her room. Instead she raced down the stairs and flew out the back door, not caring when it slammed behind her. She hopped the garden wall and marched up into the hills, feeling like a storm was raging inside her. She felt no relief that her second task was complete, that only one more stood between her and the mainland. It was a battle to keep tears from brimming over.

She kept replaying the moment when Sean had disappeared over the harbour wall. She couldn't shake the memory of Alasdair's expression when he'd looked up from the water – like he didn't know her at all. Like he couldn't believe what she'd done to him.

And now Libby was giving up on her. What had all of this been for, if she was already being forgotten back home?

Blair stuffed her fists into her jacket pockets and pushed onwards. Finally she came to the forbidding slab of granite that stood at the summit of the hill.

"Cailleach?" she called, and her voice echoed back to her from the closest crags.

"Good news, I hear," came her answer. Cailleach was seated at the top of the stone, one leg hanging over the edge, the other tucked into her chest. The sun was low behind her, silhouetting the sharp tines of her antlers. "I'm pleased. But I cannot give you the third task yet. It must wait until the dark of the moon, which, unfortunately for us both, is still a fortnight away."

Blair squinted against the last rays of sunlight. Ignoring Cailleach's words, she steeled herself. "I want out of the deal," she said.

Cailleach moved and the sun glared into Blair's eyes so brightly that she had to shut them tight. When she opened them again, Cailleach was right in front of her. Blair staggered backwards in shock.

"What did you say?" Cailleach's voice was unnervingly soft; she tilted her head to the side.

"I said I want out." Blair's hands balled into fists. "I don't want to be part of this any more. I'll find my own way home."

Cailleach watched her coolly, no trace of surprise in her ageless features. "Is that so?"

The guardian's composure threw Blair for a moment, but she gathered herself together. "My friends lost their dad just now. You made me do that!"

Cailleach only tutted, as though Blair was testing her patience. "Did I guide your hand? Your choices are your own. Thanks to you, a selkie has gained his freedom, and one more wrong caused by humans has been made right."

"I didn't sign up for this," Blair snapped. "You don't tell me anything and then you just leave me to deal with the consequences! I don't want your help any more. It's as simple as that."

"It is not, as it happens. And you did, indeed, sign up for this. See that antler on your wrist?" Cailleach pointed with one slender finger, and Blair covered the bracelet with her hand, as though shielding it from sight would make it less real.

"That is a *fey bargain*," Cailleach said, enunciating each syllable. "It cannot be broken, except by fulfilling the terms. If you run away now, you will never remove it. That antler will draw the attention of every fey creature for miles around, no matter where you go."

The sun passed behind a cloud; Blair felt a shiver travel down her back. She remembered the Bean Nighe's cold breath around her wrist, and the sharpness of the Cat-Sìth's claws when it scratched her arm.

"How much do you know about the fey folk of Roscoe, Blair Zielinski?" Cailleach asked. "Very little, as far as I can gather. You will not have heard of the Sluagh, then: some call them the restless dead. Wakeful souls that flock together like crows and turn the sky black as they gather up the spirits of those who are soon to die."

Clouds were knitting together overhead, dark and heavy. They seemed to have appeared out of nowhere. A cold wind rushed in from the sea and swept over Blair, setting her teeth on edge. It brought with it the harsh cawing of crows, many of them, growing louder.

A shadow passed over Cailleach's face. Blair lifted her eyes to the sky. A thick tangle of what looked like crows soared over them, flocking together so closely they blocked out the sun. There must have been hundreds of them, shoaling together in the shape of a crescent moon as they crossed the sky.

Their cries became louder as the birds flocked lower. One of the crows broke loose and came gliding down over their heads. Cailleach didn't flinch as the bird turned to soar between her antlers.

As the bird spun past Blair's face, a distant voice in the back of her head urged her to run – but she couldn't seem to take a single step.

"And what of the Wulver?" Cailleach went on, unmoved. The crows turned, circling high above them both. "Part man, part wolf, belonging to neither. Haunting the uplands alone."

Blair finally unglued her feet and took a step away – but then a long, mournful howl echoed from the furthest hills. Blair froze in her tracks once again and felt a prickling sensation travel along her spine.

"Once these creatures roamed the mainland, too." There was a trace of glee in Cailleach's voice. "As human belief dimmed, the fey and human realms peeled apart. But not here. Never forget that on Roscoe, the fey still hold sway."

Another howl cut through the rising wind, and this time, it was closer.

Blair turned from Cailleach and ran.

She had never known an evening as dark as this. The cacophony of the Sluagh only grew louder as she raced down the hillside in the dim light, and the howl sounded once more. Her heart hammered against her ribs, and her feet slipped on reeds and sank into bog as she tore down the moorland towards the steading.

Cailleach didn't seem to be following her, but Blair didn't dare look back. Her foot caught on a stone and she fell to her knees. When she raised her head, panting, she could see the steading in the distance. Between her and the house was a sea of treacherous bog.

There was a light: glimmering faintly at first, then gathering brightness. It glittered and shifted like distant starlight. In a brief moment of stillness, Blair saw that its body was long and slender, its wings translucent and shimmering, like a dragonfly.

A will-o'-the-wisp.

Blair picked herself up and walked straight towards it. Her feet found safe purchase with every step. By the time she reached the light, it had vanished, but another had appeared further away. She began to jog towards it, and then the next, and soon she was running flat out between the lights, surefooted on the machair.

When Blair's hands finally found the handle on the steading's back door she felt like her heart might burst. She pulled herself inside and slammed the door closed behind her, sinking to the ground with her back against it, her hands shaking.

FLEDGLING

The sky was no longer dark with flocking crow-spirits, but the sunlight did not return. Black clouds drove in from the Atlantic, blotting out the sunset. Blair watched from her bedroom window as rain sheeted over the restless sea. The wildflowers of the machair were flattened by gusts of wind battering the shore. Blair flinched as they howled around the rafters, rattling the windows in their frames.

The rain slammed into the house all at once, a thunderous cacophony on the roof and walls. Blair peered out through the rain-spattered window and saw the owl hunkered down in its nest below, the thick rushes curled up to the wall, creating a safe little haven. Blair did the same, curling herself into a protective ball beneath her duvet and blankets.

The wind and rain were deafening, but at least they drowned out Blair's despair.

A new day came and the storm finally passed, but Blair couldn't go out there and pretend everything was fine.

There was nothing else for it but to stay in bed. Alasdair wouldn't want to see her face; just thinking of him and Ewan made her chest tighten. She wished she could just empty her mind. Wished that her memory wouldn't keep dredging up Alasdair's look of disgust, Cailleach's fury, the tears on her mum's face.

Blair had never seen her mum cry before. Never.

And if she was completely honest, it wasn't just shame keeping her in bed. The howling in the hills, the awful shrieking of the crows… The previous day's events had shaken her to her core. Blair pulled the duvet up over her head and tried to fall back to sleep.

A sudden screech made her sit up straight.

Blair slipped out of the covers and padded over to the window, pressing her face against the glass.

The little owl was up and out of its nest, standing in the grass, looking away from her. It kept ruffling its feathers and adjusting its feet – it looked, in short, like it was up to something.

In the next moment, Blair was at her bedroom door, inching it open to peek outside. No one was in the kitchen. She scurried across the room and let herself out.

Bright sunshine beat down, warming the bare skin of her arms and feet. She walked around the house and there it was: the little owl, its violet eyes bright. It wiggled its head from side to side as she crept closer, keeping to the wall.

"It's all right," she said in a soothing voice. "I won't bother you."

She slid down the wall until she was squatting with her back against it. The owl's eyes were so big now that it couldn't help but look alarmed as it watched her.

But then it turned away and leapt into the air, beating its wings once, twice, then landing again. Blair gasped. The owl hadn't moved more than its own height off the ground, and it had travelled less than a metre. But when its wings were outstretched, it had transformed into a totally different creature to the little blob that now stood on the grass, looking uncertain once more.

A shadow moved across Blair's face.

"Wow," she heard her dad breathe. "A fledgling! What kind of owl is it?"

"No idea."

"Right. Don't go anywhere." He disappeared inside. Blair raised her eyebrows at the owl, who followed his progress with its bobbing head.

A few minutes later, her dad reappeared with a book in his hands. He sank down next to Blair.

A Guide to the Owls of Scotland. Of course. He began to turn the pages, glancing up at the little creature now and then to scrutinise it.

"There." Blair put her hand into the book to stop him turning the page. "Isn't that it?"

Her dad looked hard at the illustration. "You're right! A short-eared owl… They hunt by day! Imagine that!"

"Its nest is outside my window," said Blair.

Her dad looked at her in wonder, and Blair's chest flooded with warmth. "Have you seen the parents?"

She shook her head. "Never. But it seems to be doing all right. I mean – he? How do we tell?"

Her dad scanned the page. "There's a difference in the markings on the feathers. Do you have any?"

Blair tiptoed over to the nest and found a soft, fluffy feather within. She brought it over to her dad, who studied it closely. "Right... See how these lines are broken? I think that means it's female." He pointed to the markings at the lower end of the feather, thin lines beside a pattern of smudges.

"She," Blair confirmed. "So what does it mean, what you said before – that she's a fledgling?"

"It means she's developing feathers that will be strong enough for flight. She's left the nest and is starting to teach herself."

Blair couldn't stop a smile from breaking across her face. "She's trying again!" she whispered, grabbing her dad's arm. The owl launched herself into the air once more, and this time she flew as high as the garden wall, where she landed ungracefully.

Blair turned to grin at her dad, but the smile fell away – he was already looking at her, a troubled crease to his brow.

"I'm sorry you're finding it so hard," he said. "I know your phone is your lifeline. But it's not for ever."

Blair looked down into her lap.

"Moving here has been our dream for as long as you've

been alive, Blair. It's what kept us going through all the years we were scraping a living."

Blair swallowed and nodded, still unable to meet his gaze.

"Your mum… She's been wound tightly these last few years, wondering if we would ever be able to save enough to move here. Once you get in the habit of worrying all the time, it's very hard to break. You just need to give her time."

Blair let his words sink in. She looked at her dad: his unlined face, the square glasses that obscured his youthful eyes.

It had never occurred to her before that her parents were not *actually* very old. Alasdair's parents had to be a good decade older. What had Blair's parents even done before they'd had her? They had married not long after school, she knew that much. And then she'd come along. She had only ever known them working, one parent in the house while the other was on shift.

It was very possible that moving to this wild, remote place was the first thing they'd done for themselves in her entire life.

And she was one task away from destroying it.

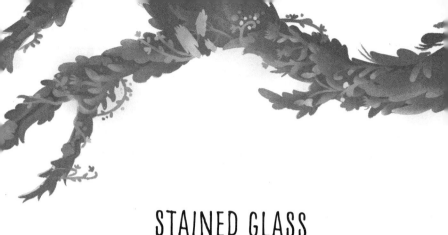

STAINED GLASS

Every morning Blair woke with an anxious knot in her stomach, imagining Cailleach's antlered silhouette watching her house from the hills. There was nothing she could do but wait and worry about what Cailleach's final task would entail.

The memory of that dark mass of crows flocking together, transforming a summer's evening into night, still gave Blair shivers. *We need the dark of the moon*, Cailleach had said. Blair had asked her dad what that meant: the new moon, when the moon moved between the earth and the sun, leaving the nights dark. Cailleach had said it was a fortnight away – but what would happen then was anyone's guess.

She wasn't going to learn anything from her room. At least in the village, speaking to people, she might pick up some clues…

It had been over a week since her crafternoon with Rosemary. The old woman was due a visit.

The fresh air rushing over the handlebars brought with it a sense of relief as Blair cycled down the road towards the village. The cloud had lifted in more ways than one; the sun was scorching, and Blair suspected her face might be a little sunburnt by the time she reached Fraoch. Morag answered the door in a floral dress.

"Blair Zielinski! Mother's been asking after you. How are those parents of yours? We're all dying to see what they've done with the place. The inspection can't come soon enough! And your father told me he's going to treat us all to an authentic Polish meal afterwards."

"He did?" This was news to Blair. It sounded like bribery – but her dad's cooking was the best in the world, so it was likely to work.

"Oh, yes. Bigos, I think he called it. I must say, I'm very excited."

Blair stepped into the hallway as Morag rolled back to let her in.

"Is Rosemary home?" she asked.

"Of course. Go on up!"

The door to the attic room was already open when Blair reached it, but she knocked all the same. Rosemary hastily snapped shut the sketchbook she had been drawing in.

"It's my favourite spy. Survived the storm, did you?"

"Just about," Blair said. "What are you working on today? Doesn't look like you're going to need my help." She nodded to the sketchbook.

"You'd be surprised," Rosemary answered.

Blair realised what the old woman was holding in her trembling hand – what she'd been drawing with. A black marker! Blair's trademark.

"Can I see?" she asked excitedly, reaching for the sketchbook. Rosemary held it out of her reach.

"I don't think so, lass – this isn't exactly my speciality. But lend me yours, would you? I want to check how you do your flowers."

Blair dug her sketchbook out of her bag and handed it over.

Rosemary flipped through Blair's sketchbook until she found the page she was looking for. She began sketching quickly, copying Blair's drawing of red clover stroke for stroke.

Blair took the opportunity to wander the makeshift gallery. Every one of Rosemary's artworks seemed to tell a story.

Her toe caught on a cardboard-wrapped package leaning against the wall, and glass crunched. Blair gasped.

"Relax, it's broken already," Rosemary said without looking back.

Still, Blair kneeled down and unfolded the cardboard to reveal the contents. It was a pane of glass, and it was already, clearly, shattered in several places. But where she had tripped, the corner of the pane had broken again.

"I'm so sorry," she said, and Rosemary shushed her.

"What's one more break to repair? Don't worry. It's the push I needed. I've had that pane far too long already."

"It's from the pub," Blair said, realisation dawning. It was the missing first pane from the trio of stained glass images. The man who had been striding into the loch in the second pane was depicted here, on the right-hand half of the image. He wore a tartan kilt in dark maroon over his furred brown legs. His cloven hooves were planted in the turf; he looked like a giant against the backdrop of the hills. A constellation of deer were scattered across them.

The main break in the pane was along a silver join in the centre of the image – and illustrated on the other side was Cailleach.

There was no mistaking her: the long, wild hair, the rust-red dress belted with cord, and above all, the crown of antlers.

She was facing the man; they were looking at each other. But who was he?

"Bodach," Rosemary said, as if she had read Blair's mind. "Bodach and Cailleach, the great guardians of the deer."

The hairs on Blair's arms rose. *In a time of great change, Bodach abandoned us. I have been trying to protect Roscoe alone ever since.* Blair remembered Cailleach's words clearly, but they meant as little to her now as they had then.

"What does it mean?" Blair breathed, eyes roving over every detail of the image. "How do the panes fit together?"

Rosemary only sighed deeply and got to her feet. "Tea?"

Blair hardly heard her, but she must have replied, because Rosemary left the room.

Cailleach said Bodach had abandoned her and the fey, but why – to become that deer creature? The giant stag that had risen out of the loch in the final window pane – the monster that Morag had called the Fiadh Mho'r? Why would he leave Cailleach and their deer behind?

Blair turned for her sketchbook and saw that Rosemary's copy of her red clover was perfect. Not only that, but she'd been sketching a whale on the opposite page – there were close-ups of its tail fluke and the patterns of black and white around its face. Helpfully, she had inscribed *Orca* in the bottom right-hand corner.

Blair rolled her eyes. The old woman could turn her hand to anything.

She uncapped her marker and did a quick sketch of the stained glass illustration. When she heard Rosemary's footsteps on the stairs she flipped the page back and jumped into her seat by the workbench.

Rosemary set down a steaming mug in front of Blair. "This is dandelion root tea – my very own brew."

Blair wrinkled her nose. "Dandelion?"

"Don't knock it 'til you've tried it."

Rosemary sat down with her own cup, gazing absently out of the window. The boat house was visible around the curve in the narrow road. "Terrible what's happened to the Reid family," she remarked.

Blair felt her cheeks heating. "What do you mean?"

"You don't know?" Rosemary paused for a weighted moment, then went on, "I thought you and Alasdair were becoming friends?"

"I – um, I haven't seen him for a few days. What's going on?"

"I heard Sean Reid left, and it's a dreadful shame. I thought he was a good man."

Blair swallowed.

"You can imagine what folk on this island are saying about it, of course," Rosemary went on.

Blair just shook her head, distracted by the guilt swelling in her chest.

"Well, since our island's *haunted* and all, they're saying Sean never left. They're saying he was taken by the Fiadh Mho'r."

"The Sea Stag," Blair said.

"Aye. That's ridiculous, of course, since the Fiadh Mho'r's never caused harm to man nor beast, except at the new moon." Rosemary glanced at her sidelong.

Blair couldn't just sit around and wait to see what Cailleach was going to throw at her. She needed to repair the damage that had already been done.

First things first: she needed to find Sean Reid.

Blair grabbed a tourist map from the leaflet stand in the hallway at Fraoch on her way home. It was flimsy, and nowhere near as detailed as Alasdair's, but it did indicate every path on the small island.

That evening, she spread the map out on her bed and pored over it. If Aileen and Sean had met on the island, it seemed very likely that he had lived in the sea around here as a seal. So he may not be far away at all.

Casting her mind back to the time she'd gone up to Alasdair and Ewan's bedroom, Blair remembered the hand-drawn map on the wall that had indicated where different species could be found. Seals had been marked in one spot in particular: a curved bay.

She scanned the edges of the island. The coastline was so jagged, there were bays everywhere.

There was only one thing for it. She'd have to start at her front door and work her way around.

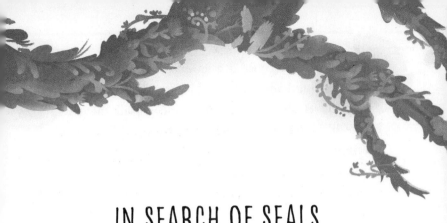

IN SEARCH OF SEALS

The next morning, while her parents were busy assembling furniture upstairs, Blair gathered her supplies and headed east. There was a path hollowed out of the sandy turf beside the shore, and there was no getting lost as long as she kept the sea to her right.

The path rose steadily up until she was walking along the clifftops, a light chill on the Atlantic wind. To her right, the turf dropped away suddenly to crystal-blue water peppered with white crests and black rocks. To her left, springy grass raced out to meet coarse heather and shining bog, rolling upwards into the Creachanns.

She noticed that two birds had been flying overhead for a while now: a puffin and a tern, just like the day she'd searched the village with Alasdair. She tried to ignore them, but their presence was unnerving.

Blair ate her lunch while scanning the sea for seals, but was startled when a huge spray of water puffed out from the surface. She heard a sound like a great exhalation and jumped to her feet just as a tall black fin sliced through the waves. Suddenly the animal leapt up out of the water and came crashing down. Blair recognised the curve of the black body, the white patches, from Rosemary's sketchbook.

Orca.

She really was in another world.

The following day dawned bright and clear. Blair's dad was repainting the whitewash on the house when she wheeled her bike out.

There was a familiar screech, and they both turned their faces upward. The short-eared owl was perched on the ridge of the roof, head rotating this way and that. She looked less of a fluffy fledgling now; her feathers were the colour of coffee cake flecked with cream, black tufts at her tail. Her violet eyes glowed in a white-framed face that was the shape of an apple sliced in half.

She threw out her wings, soared over their heads and turned for the machair, flying low over the wildflowers – hunting.

"She needs a name," Blair's dad mused. "What about Osag? It's Gaelic for a gust of wind."

He was watching the owl so intently he hadn't noticed that white paint was dripping onto his shoe.

Blair hummed. "We'll keep workshopping."

It wasn't long before she was cycling through the village, glancing up at the boat house as she passed by.

She bumped over the harbour cobbles, another few miles past cottages and smallholdings, right to the very end of the road. Then she left her bike on the verge and continued on foot.

The winding western path led her up a steep slope until she was walking along another sheer cliffside. Her boots crunched on the gravel underfoot and her breath came quickly as she trudged onwards.

At first she thought there was a pile of bleached white stones up ahead. But as she drew closer, Blair realised she was looking at a spinal column of unimaginable size, the wings of the vertebrae as long as her arm. *Whale bones.* Someone had to have dragged them up here from the shore a long time ago, for the spine seemed to be the only part of the skeleton left and the bones were picked clean.

Blair ran her hands over the rough surface of the plane of bone, her antler bracelet clacking against it, like to like.

The spine suddenly trembled beneath her hand.

Blair snatched her hand away, and her mouth fell open in shock as the surface of the bone shivered and began to move. A hundred creatures, all the same bleached white, started scuttling sideways: *crabs.*

Blair let out a yell so loud all the nearby seabirds scattered, but she hardly noticed, because she was already darting towards the path that led down the cliffside.

She ran until the giant's skeleton was out of sight beyond the rise, glancing back over her shoulder. It didn't seem like she was being followed by an army of crabs.

She took a few steps back along the path and peeked

over the clifftop. She hadn't imagined it: the crabs were still there, standing on their spindly white legs on top of the vertebrae. But where they had emerged there was a fracture in the bone – and from it emanated a strangely familiar silver glow.

A moment later the crabs scuttled back into place, and the whalebone was reformed as seamlessly as though they had never existed. Blair shuddered as the scene settled into stillness once again.

Her foot slipped on a loose pebble, and Blair nearly swayed with vertigo when she realised how high the cliffs were, how narrow the trail was.

But below her, a crescent moon of sand was hidden away beneath the cliffs, and azure waves lapped peacefully at the shore. The sand was covered in shapes like speckled grey-blue stones, but they were wriggling and rolling and bouncing along on their bellies.

Seals.

Dozens upon dozens of seals, loudly enjoying the sunshine. Blair felt herself smiling from ear to ear. Some of them were making long, melodious sounds, almost like singing, which others interrupted with a bark.

Blair stood still for a long time, spellbound. She watched them interacting with each other, basking in the sun, flopping back into the water. She couldn't think of a time in her life when she had seen so many wild creatures at once.

How many of them were selkies? Any? All? How was she to know?

The sun caught on the seals' skins with a silvery gleam. And then it struck her where she had seen that strange glow in the bone before: it was the same ethereal shade as the sealskin she and Ewan had discovered in the shed.

Whatever the crabs were guarding, it had something to do with selkies.

Swallowing unhappily, Blair turned back to the bones.

This time, when the antler bracelet brushed the spine of what had once been a whale, Blair didn't move. When the bone shivered and the crabs scuttled aside, she gritted her teeth and let them rush past her. They pooled around her hands in a clacking, wavering oval around the bones, but then they waited.

Blair turned her attention to what they had been concealing. Against the greying marrow was a long, carved line filled with the silver that had caught the light. Blair glanced up at the beach ahead. The carving was an outline of the bay and the cliffs surrounding it. It was a *map*.

At the far end of the bay, the northernmost end, was the symbol of a face: one side human, one side seal, split down the middle by a thin line.

Blair looked past the map in the bones, down at the crescent of sand. At the far end of the bay, reddish cliffs stretched out into the turquoise water.

This was where she'd find the selkies.

The steep, narrow path zigzagged back and forth down the cliffside. Blair picked her way down it, sending rocks tumbling.

When she hit the sand, she set off at a run. Her sudden movement startled the nearest seals, who startled their neighbours, until the whole beach was rippling with motion. Seals barked and groaned and hauled themselves off the sand, turning suddenly graceful as they snaked away through the water.

By the time Blair reached the far end of the crescent of beach, there was barely a seal left on the shore. She felt terrible for disturbing them; it didn't seem like a great start.

As she caught her breath, she studied the rocky cliffside: no sign of a cave entrance or a door. She squinted out at the cerulean sea where it lapped against the rocks.

She hadn't swum in the sea since she was small.

But there was no question of turning back. She needed to find Sean. She needed to show Alasdair that she was sorry. She couldn't imagine finding the courage to face her final task without him. Exploring the island had almost started to feel like fun when they were together. It had almost started to feel like... home.

Blair kicked off her shoes and dropped her backpack onto the sand, rolling her trousers up to her knees. She took a deep breath and waded into the water.

It was chilly, but quite a relief after her run. The sand sloped away, and it wasn't long before water was splashing at the rolls of her trousers. She carried on wading anyway, letting the seawater soak her through. Her heart picked up speed as she moved deeper, but she kept her feet firmly planted on the ground as waves lapped gently at her middle.

Blair hugged the rocky base of the cliff, feeling along the rough stone with her hands in case they revealed anything she couldn't see. When she was submerged to her chest she realised she would have to turn back. She was alone, and she wasn't prepared to swim without anyone watching from the shore. But who exactly was that supposed to be?

She pushed on a few steps further until the waves reached her collarbone. It was just far enough to round an outcrop of rock, and on the other side there was a low, wide opening. A cave.

She took a step and her toes scuffed at the sand, only just making contact. But she was in the mouth of the cave, and she saw that there were carvings in the stone overhead. A symbol that matched the one from the map: a face, half-human, half-seal. There were a few words inscribed in Gaelic, but of course she couldn't read them.

Blair stared into the dark mouth of the cave and chewed on her bottom lip. Then she took a deep breath and plunged forward.

The water pushed back. Instead of entering the cave, Blair found herself inexplicably facing out to sea. She was treading water now, her toes barely brushing the sand.

She swam into the mouth of the cave again, and once more she was turned away. Literally turned back, as though a giant invisible hand had guided her out.

She needed to be sure. Blair approached once again, and this time, she saw a pair of flashing eyes in the darkness beyond. She was so startled she gulped a mouthful of seawater, and her ears filled with the sound of hissing. A second pair of eyes appeared, and a third.

"I'm a friend," Blair said, her heart hammering. The eyes didn't come closer, but they didn't move away. The hissing only grew louder.

Blair swam back to the shallows, and once her feet had found purchase she looked back towards the cave, her heart rate slowly returning to normal.

She had found where the selkies lived. They may not want her there, but she had found them, and that was something.

Besides, it seemed that whatever magic controlled the cave entrance meant that she wasn't permitted to enter.

But maybe she knew someone who would be.

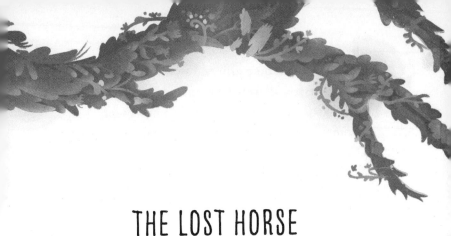

THE LOST HORSE

Blair was crossing the bridge over the river when she thought she heard her name being called. She had half a mind to go to the boat house right now, but it was already late in the afternoon so maybe it'd be best to wait until morning. The sooner she could make things right with Alasdair, the sooner she could confess everything, and start to prepare—

"Blair! *Blair!* KELPIE HUNTER!"

Her name *was* being called. She slammed the brakes on her bike and looked around, but there was only Mr Okafor outside the general store, bringing in the shop's wares from the pavement.

"Down *here*," the voice said, sounding exasperated.

Blair got off her bike and looked over the side of the bridge. She peered down at the water rushing along the riverbed, but there didn't seem to be anyone there. Then Irving's face broke the surface, grinning. They were floating on their back, and an otter was resting on their chest. It ran down their arm and swam off into the water.

"Why are you all wet? Get dunked by another kelpie?" Irving asked, mouth downturned in amusement.

"Something like that," Blair said. "Were you looking for me?"

"Did calling your name repeatedly give it away? *Yes*, I was looking for you. I've been hoping you'd come back for days, but apparently they don't teach you about aftercare in kelpie-hunter training."

"Aftercare?" Blair repeated. "You mean… the kelpie? It's still there?"

Irving hopped up onto the riverbank. Blair wheeled her bike off the bridge and left it on the grass as she joined the river guardian, who was shaking droplets out of their hair.

"It just won't *leave*. Everything's too afraid to move for fear of being chomped."

Blair felt a surge of guilt just as Irving grabbed hold of her sleeve and began towing her along the riverbank path with surprising force. Blair pried herself free.

"You don't need to drag me, all right? I'm coming. I'm sorry – I didn't mean to saddle you all with it."

Irving waved her apologies away. "It's just to reassure the trout. I mean, *I* was never in any danger, but I still don't like having an uninvited guest lurking around the place."

Blair had to jog every other step to keep up with the pace Irving was setting. "How come you weren't in danger?"

Irving glanced back at her and wrinkled their nose.

"I forget how little you humans know sometimes. No fey creature can harm another. That's a sure-fire way to land a curse on your head."

"A curse?" Blair repeated. "I didn't realise there were rules to being fey."

"Oh, we've got rules coming out of our ears," Irving drawled. "A guardian can never harm the thing we protect; but then again, why would you? Do I look like I want to eat a fish? It'd be like you taking a bite out of your brother."

Blair stored that information away for later. "I don't have a brother. But I get your point."

"The kelpie, though, he isn't a guardian, like me. Not a protector of anything, just a hunter. They only look out for themselves. So they can prey on *my* non-fey friends, and I can't do anything about it."

"But he's stopped now, right? He's just a horse?"

"Oh yeah. But try telling that to the dippers when he's still looming over the river."

At the speed they were moving, it took no time at all to reach the pool Blair had been tossed into by the kelpie.

And there he was, cropping grass on the riverbank, the whites of his eyes showing as he watched them from afar. A living reminder that Blair was already two tasks down, and the clock was ticking on the third. Her chest tightened at the sight of him.

"Right, thanks then," Irving said breezily. "Do your thing."

Without another word, Irving stepped into the river and disappeared beneath the surface.

"The fey folk are so helpful," Blair muttered. At the sound of her voice, the horse lifted his head. His whole body went rigid, and his ears kept telescoping at the slightest noise.

He was afraid.

Blair felt the tension in her body soften. When she took a step towards him he leaned back as though poised to leap away at any moment. Blair took a deep breath and let it out slowly.

"It's okay," she said in the most soothing tone she could manage. "It's good to see you again. I'm glad you're a vegetarian these days, that's for sure."

It was nonsense, but the horse seemed to be reassured by her outstretched hand and the calming notes of her voice, lowering his head.

Blair ventured a step closer. His head bobbed up again, but he didn't move away. She reached her hand out and felt his warm, damp breath on her knuckles.

"We're fine," Blair said. She looked him over without moving her body too much: his tangled black mane, his soft brown hair, his black hooves. Two of his lower legs had white stripes, and these ran down into the pigment of his hooves. The bump where the base of his neck met his back was about the same height as her shoulders, and with his head raised his nose was level with her chin.

Blair kept her hand steady until he touched it with his nose, and then she flattened her palm over his soft muzzle. When the antler bracelet bumped against his nose he startled, nostrils flaring in alarm.

Blair tucked the bracelet carefully into her sleeve, then placed her hand against his cheek. She worked her way up the side of his furry jaw until she was stroking the hair of his neck.

When she was small, her mum had sometimes lifted her up to stroke the horses in the fields outside Carlisle. A feeling she couldn't name rose within her: something protective.

"I don't know what I'm supposed to do with you, but you can't stay here," she said gently. "Let's try something."

She lowered her hand, turned back towards the village, and began to walk.

The kelpie-horse fell into step behind her.

Blair laughed as she looked back over her shoulder. The horse was following like a faithful dog.

Maybe if she led him to the village and left him hanging around there someone would take him in. But she couldn't deny how it warmed her heart to have the huge creature following in her footsteps.

When they reached the bridge, a bluish hand stuck out of the water in a thumbs-up.

"You're welcome," Blair grumbled. The sun was sinking low in the sky; she'd be late for dinner, and she was still damp from the sea. She picked up her bike and mounted.

"You stay here, okay?" she urged the horse, who had stopped to snap blades of grass from the verge. But when she set off into the road the horse followed, his hooves clattering on the cobbles.

What would people think if they looked out their

windows and saw the strange new girl leading a horse around like the Pied Piper?

Past the village, Blair pedalled slowly, since the horse was still behind her. Fortunately, he didn't come out into the road, but trotted along through the machair beside her. When she sped up, so did he, breaking into a lolloping canter. She laughed with joy.

All she'd intended to do today was find the selkies, and now she was bringing a former kelpie home.

How exactly was she going to explain this one?

As she drew close to the steading, she realised with dismay that both her parents were in the front garden, painting the old stables. They must have heard the hoofbeats, because one by one they turned, shielding their eyes against the afternoon sun. Her dad's shoulders began to shake with laughter.

When Blair stepped through the garden gate, the horse stayed on the far side. He was puffing, his big sides heaving, nostrils wide. He dropped his head and began to graze, keeping his eyes fixed on the three of them.

Blair searched for the words and failed.

"Are there wild horses on the island?" her dad asked. "I've never heard of any!"

"I think there's … just one." Blair gestured helplessly to the animal. "I was walking by the river. He followed me all the way home!"

Her mum had her arms folded across her chest, but there was a smile twitching at her lips.

"I'm sure he'll head back in his own time," her dad said.

"I suppose it's common land. No reason why he shouldn't graze out here."

"As long as he keeps off the road," Blair's mum said.

Blair was astonished that this hadn't kicked off an argument. Her mum walked up to the wall, held out her hand for the horse to sniff and then patted him familiarly on the neck. Blair could hardly believe what she was seeing.

All the while, their violet-eyed owl watched curiously from the ridge of the roof.

THOSE OF SELKIE BLOOD

The horse had not left by the following morning. He was grazing amongst the wildflowers on the machair, but Blair watched him from an upstairs window and noted that his body was always oriented towards the house, at least one eye keeping the steading in view.

Blair glanced at the hills behind him, at the standing stone where she had first met Cailleach. She wondered if the deer guardian was watching her now, and shivered.

When she came downstairs she found her mum filling a bucket under the kitchen tap. "What are you doing?" Blair asked.

"I'm going to take him some water."

"There's a stream right next to the house!"

"Well, he might want it anyway."

Blair held the door open for her mum as she walked out, water splashing over the sides of the bucket. Blair shook her head. She had more important things to be worrying about today.

She got her stuff together, including the large roll of thick paper that constituted the previous night's work. The horse seemed to be distracted by her mum's offering: he had his nose stuck in the bucket and was sloshing it around, snorting bubbles, while Blair's mum laughed.

That was good. The last thing Blair needed was a horse trailing her.

It was still early by the time she reached the boat house, but she was relieved to see that the car usually parked out the front was gone. Her palms were damp as she approached, her mind swimming with guilt.

Blair knocked on the door, then wrapped her arms tightly around herself. Eventually a porthole creaked open overhead.

Alasdair stuck his head out and frowned heavily. "Oh. It's you." He pulled the window shut.

Blair knocked on the door more insistently this time. The window opened again.

"Leave. Us. Alone!"

"I need to talk to you! It's about your dad!"

"We don't want anything to do with you!" Alasdair yelled and slammed the window closed.

Blair hesitated on the doorstep, unsure whether it was a good idea to try a third time. A black-headed gull above the porch screeched loudly at Blair as though it was angry with her too. She flinched away, but then her breath caught and she peered closer.

The gull's eyes were violet, like her owl's.

The front door opened slowly.

It was Ewan, his face tear-stained and shining. "What about Dad?"

Alasdair came thundering down the stairs and into the hallway. "Don't listen to her, Ewan." He tried to usher him away from the door, but Blair spoke first.

"I know where he is!"

Alasdair froze. He looked up at Blair slowly, and behind the hurt in his eyes she saw the faintest shred of hope.

"Really," Blair said. Quickly she unzipped her backpack and pulled out the paper. Alasdair snatched it from her and hastily unrolled it.

"What is this supposed to be?" he asked.

She thought that was fairly obvious, but okay. It was a stylised map of the island, all the main waterways and hills marked with winding lines and sharp triangles, a few animal symbols where she had spotted them. But the coastline was the focus, every inlet and headland copied meticulously from the tourist map, and Whalebone Bay was marked with a big X.

"It's the island. And that's where your dad is. I think."

"You think?"

"Well I didn't actually *see* him—" Blair began, and Alasdair moved to shut the door in her face, but she threw out her arm to stop him. "Alasdair, listen to me! I found a cave there. There were carvings; I think they meant it was a place for selkies. I couldn't enter. They didn't want me to."

Alasdair lowered the map so that Ewan could get a look at it too. His brow was heavy, his mouth twisted, but he was studying the map closely. "Whalebone Bay," he murmured. "He takes us there sometimes. To see the seals."

"I think you'll find him there," Blair said, beginning to step back. "Maybe you can speak to him. Maybe he'll come home."

Alasdair seemed to be engrossed in his thoughts; she wasn't sure he had heard her. She began to turn away.

"Wait."

She looked back over her shoulder. Alasdair was looking straight at her, and the anger in his face had softened slightly. "You should come with us."

Once Alasdair and Ewan were appropriately kitted out for the expedition, they set off. Blair led the way to the coastal path and along the cliffs. Alasdair walked a few steps behind her, holding Ewan's hand. There was plenty of room for them all to walk side by side, but she got the message.

"I'm glad I caught you before you left for your survey," she called back.

"I'm not doing the survey right now," Alasdair said gruffly. "Someone has to look after Ewan."

Blair's face fell, but fortunately she had her back to the boys. "Oh."

It was almost noon by the time they reached Whalebone Bay. The wind was high, clouds chasing each other across the sky, and the water didn't look quite as calm and inviting as it had the day before. There were half as many seals on the sand today, but plenty of heads bobbing in the water.

Ewan clung to the hem of Alasdair's jumper. "Is Dad there?"

"I don't know. Let's see."

Blair led the way down the crumbling cliffside path with a wary glance at the whalebones.

The seals didn't take fright as they passed today; some of them lifted their heads to watch them go, bodies curled like fat grey bananas.

The tide was further out than it had been the last time, which would work in their favour. Blair had been hoping she would be invited along, so today she was prepared: she stripped off her clothes until she was standing in nothing but shorts and a rash vest she'd borrowed from her mum. She'd also pilfered a head torch from the cupboard.

Ewan pulled off his T-shirt and handed Blair two pieces of rubbery plastic. "Can you do these?"

Blair started blowing up the inflatable armbands, turning away as Alasdair pulled off his jumper. When she'd helped Ewan fit them onto his arms, Alasdair was standing in a T-shirt and shorts, shivering, with his arms folded tightly over his chest. Blair remembered what he'd told her by the river: *I don't swim.*

"Follow me," Blair said, and walked out into the sea.

Alasdair lifted Ewan onto his hip and waded into the water. The cave wasn't out of Blair's depth any more, but she was still in above her waist when they approached the entrance, and the water was choppier. Ewan shrieked whenever a wave lapped at his feet, but he went quiet when Blair pointed to the carvings in the stone.

"Open to those of selkie blood," Alasdair mumbled, and Blair realised he was translating the Gaelic.

"That's why I couldn't enter," she mused aloud.

Alasdair nodded slowly. "Are we of selkie blood, then?"

"One way to find out."

Alasdair looked at Ewan and adjusted his brother's weight on his hip. "Here goes nothing." He waded forwards. The cave did not turn them away; they stepped through as though there were no barrier at all. Alasdair turned back to face Blair.

"I didn't even get that far," she told him. His eyes lit up.

"So we *can* enter." He chewed his lip thoughtfully, then held out a hand. "Come with us."

Blair felt a flutter in her chest as she reached towards him. Their fingers touched, then locked together, and when she stepped forward into the cave she closed her eyes, but she met no resistance. When she opened them again she was standing side by side with the boys beneath the overhanging rock.

Alasdair smiled and dropped her hand. "Wasn't sure that would work," he admitted.

Blair clicked on her torch, turning to face the dark depths of the cave. She squared her shoulders. "Let's find your dad."

Blair could feel her heartbeat quickening as they were swallowed by the inky blackness. It was only just tall enough for her to stand, only wide enough for her to stretch her hands to either side and keep contact with the slimy rock. The tunnel curved away in front of them so they could never see far ahead.

"Where are they?" Alasdair whispered.

As if in answer, there was a long, low hiss – so quiet at first it could have been the water – but Blair remembered it, and a shiver ran over her shoulders.

The hiss grew louder and louder. Gradually, it took on the shape of echoing words, but Blair couldn't understand them.

"*You are not welcome,*" Alasdair translated, but his voice shook. "Blair, what if – what if it isn't the selkies?"

Blair's torch flashed on a pair of wide eyes that glowed like lamps before they disappeared around the bend. Blair swallowed. Something smooth and slick brushed past her leg, moving quickly. She stifled a yell.

"Something touched my toe!" Ewan screeched, throwing his arms around Alasdair's neck.

The hissing picked up again, only now it seemed to be coming from every direction at once. They were surrounded – Blair saw pairs of eyes whichever way she turned. Then they rose up from the water: not seals, but humans, unclothed and furious-faced. Ahead of them was what seemed to be a teenage girl with seaweed tangled in her black hair; behind them, a broad man with a red beard.

The girl said something in a grating, firm voice.

"*Humans are not welcome here,*" Alasdair translated in a low murmur.

"Tell them Sean's your dad!" Blair blurted, trying to keep both the strangers in sight, which meant she had to keep swinging the torch back and forth.

Alasdair spoke in Gaelic, but she heard the name *Sean Reid*. The girl shook her head.

"She says they don't have names," Alasdair whispered. He swallowed and spoke again, then explained to Blair: "I told her he's just returned. That he's been away a long time."

The girl said something to the man, and he nodded and sank below the surface. Blair tried not to cry out as she felt something move past her legs again.

While the man was gone, the girl watched them without expression, hardly moving. The moments stretched out; Blair couldn't say how long it had been before they heard the sound of splashing, and a familiar voice calling out around the bend, "Alasdair! Ewan!"

"Dad!"

"DAD!"

Sean came running into the torchlight, throwing up his hands against the brightness, then grinning through his fingers as he saw his sons. He looked very different from when they had seen him last – shells in his hair, bare-chested. He said something to the girl and she melted away into the depths of the cave.

Sean ran to his sons and squeezed them in a long, damp hug. "I'm sorry, my boys. I'm sorry. I'm so happy you found me." He kissed them each on the head.

"Blair found you," Alasdair said. "She brought us here."

Blair smiled sheepishly. She was worried about what she would see on Sean's face, but there was nothing but joy. She was relieved when he said, "Thank you, Blair," and didn't try to pull her into the soggy hug as well.

"Come inside and let's talk. Including you, Blair. I've got a lot of explaining to do."

He took Ewan from Alasdair and led them deeper into the dark. In only a few moments they reached a great stone cavern. Pinpricks of gold and cobalt dotted the roof overhead like constellations, reflected in still pools of water on the ground. The rock was curiously smooth and rippled, as though it had been shaped over centuries by the tides. At the edge, where the lip of the rock met the water, there were polished divots the exact shape of a seal's belly that formed slides into the sea.

There were only a few selkies present, all in human form, but they picked up their luminous silver skins and slipped into the water without a word.

"Sorry," Sean said as he lifted Ewan onto the rock. "They're pretty wary of humans."

Alasdair clambered up onto the lip and helped Blair up after him. She looked around the cave in wonder: it was eerily beautiful. Sean grabbed a pair of shorts from a shelf in the stone and pulled them on, and they sat down together in a circle.

Ewan settled himself on his dad's knee. "Why didn't they know your name, Dad?" he asked.

"It's just not something we do," Sean said. "Most selkies spend little time in human form, so we don't use names.

It was only when I started going up to the village regularly to see your mum that I realised I was going to need one. I had to choose my own! We know all about that, don't we, Alasdair? No easy task. But I settled on Sean because I liked the shape of it. And I took your mum's surname, Reid, when we got married."

"And then she hid your skin and trapped you," said Alasdair curtly.

"Well, now. Yes and no. I thought I'd lost it. But then I used to say, 'I hope I never find it.' Stupid things like that. I loved – love – your mum very much, you know. She must have taken me at my word. Perhaps she thought she was doing me a favour. But as time went by, I began to wish very much that I had never lost it. I never said that to her. I didn't want her to think that I didn't want to be with you all. If I had just said as much, maybe it all would have turned out differently."

"When are you coming home?" Ewan demanded.

"I don't know," Sean said in a low voice. "The first few days, under the waves again after so many years – I barely remembered who I was. I was just so happy to be with my folk again, in the world where I grew up. It was overwhelming."

Listening to him speak, Blair could almost feel it herself. She found herself thinking about Carlisle: her house, her school, her friends. She tried to imagine how she would feel when the tasks were done and she and her parents returned to the mainland; she was so close now, after all. She knew she ought to feel triumphant, relieved, *happy*…

but she couldn't seem to conjure those emotions at all.

"I just don't know what to do. I've missed you so much." There was a helplessness in Sean's voice that Blair wasn't used to hearing from grown-ups. It made her uncomfortable, because it made her wonder if her parents sometimes felt this way too. Weren't they supposed to have it all figured out?

"Well, we're here now," Alasdair said, his voice pleading. "Will you come home, please?"

Sean held Alasdair's gaze, something flickering behind his eyes that Blair couldn't name. "Give me time, son," he said softly. "Just give me time."

ISLAND MUSIC

They trudged back in silence along the coastal path. Emotions were warring in Blair's chest: relief that she'd reunited the family, guilt that she'd put them in this situation in the first place, and no small amount of apprehension about what lay ahead. She hadn't been able to look at Ewan and Alasdair's faces when their dad told them he still wasn't ready to choose. But at least he wasn't going to be out of their lives for ever.

Eventually Alasdair jogged up alongside her, bumping her shoulder in a friendly way. "Thanks for finding him," he said. "I was too depressed to even think of looking."

Blair's cheeks flushed. "It was the least I could do. Alasdair... I'm so sorry, about everything. I'll make it up to all of you. I promise."

Alasdair nodded, smiling faintly. They walked on in silence, but now it felt easier, more companionable.

"What was it like to choose your own name?" Blair asked.

Alasdair's eyebrows lifted in surprise, but he didn't snap at her. Instead he pursed his lips thoughtfully for a few moments. "It didn't feel like choosing," he said at last. "I mean, I was *looking*, but it was more like I discovered it. Like it was waiting. I knew I'd found my true name. The one I was meant to have." He looked at her sidelong. "Have you always felt like a Blair?" he asked, and she sensed it was just as personal a question as the one she had asked him. She thought for a moment.

"Yes," she said, surprised to discover this. "Yes, I always have."

It was early evening by the time they reached the boat house again. Blair saw the curtains twitch – Aileen was peering out at them. Alasdair caught her off guard by pulling her into a hug.

"I'm going to tell you everything," Blair said against his shoulder. "Can I come back tomorrow?"

She felt Alasdair nod. "Come by in the morning, after ten o'clock. Mum'll be at work by then."

Blair squeezed him tight and let go. She ruffled Ewan's hair, but he grabbed her around the middle and stayed there for a moment. She made a show of trying to take a big step and he giggled, then ran off.

A great, splintering *crack* from the other side of the street made Blair spin around. The wooden board that had been in place of the first window pane at the Sea Stag Inn was cleaved in two. Blair walked closer, then jumped as the thud of a sledgehammer sent half the board flying into the road. She found herself looking into the ruddy, weathered face of the tweed-clad man who ran the pub. Her parents had pointed him out before because, of course, he was on the committee.

"Stand back, lass!" he called, and she did so. The sledgehammer swung and the remainder of the wooden board clattered to the pavement. Assuming it was safe to approach now, Blair picked up the two halves and leaned them against the wall. The man had ducked out of sight, but when he reappeared, he was bearing the weight of the stained glass panel from Rosemary's studio.

"She finally fixed it!" Blair exclaimed.

The man smiled. "So she did, and just in time for the festival! At long last, Cailleach and Bodach are reunited."

He levered the panel into the window, cutting himself off from view. Blair watched the panel shuffle as it was fixed in place. Every break had been carefully soldered back together, some invisibly, others in an obvious but beautiful way with silver seams. Together, illuminated by the light from within, the three stained glass panels seemed to come to life.

Blair gazed at the story unfolding on the glass and felt unease brewing in the pit of her stomach.

At ten o'clock sharp the next morning, Alasdair answered the door before Blair had even finished knocking.

"We've just made scones. Come in."

The house was filled with the scent of fresh baking; Blair followed her nose to the kitchen table and sat down.

Ewan was attempting to butter a steaming scone with a knife that was far too large for him. Alasdair took over, taking half for himself. "Want some?"

Blair filled hers with jam; the scone was rich and warm.

"Right, then," Alasdair said with his mouth full. "Let's hear it."

Blair held up a finger and polished off her scone in two big bites. "So, I was feeling really homesick and miserable. It was right after I met you, as a matter of fact…"

Alasdair turned pink, but he listened without interrupting as she told her story, his eyebrows inching higher and higher. When she got to the part with the Sluagh and the Wulver, he began shaking his head so vigorously she was forced to stop.

"Are you all right?"

His head continued to shake. "I don't like the sound of this. Not one bit."

"But the will-o'-the-wisps helped me! I hadn't got to that part yet. And I never *saw* the Wulver, just heard it."

"The Wulver's nice," Ewan interrupted, then took a big bite of his scone. Both Alasdair and Blair turned to stare at him.

"What?" said Alasdair.

Crumbs sprayed from Ewan's mouth as he answered. "In Granddad's song, the Wulver is nice. He helps people."

"Oh yeah, your tape. It was playing when I was babysitting," Blair said. "I forgot – there was a song about Cailleach!"

Alasdair disappeared from the room and returned

with the tape player. "You're right," he said as he hit the button to rewind. The shrill squeaking made Blair jump, but Alasdair was clearly used to the noise. "Cailleach and Bodach. I've heard it a hundred times, but I've never properly listened to it."

He hit play and a strain of violin music rose from the little device.

"In the cave of the wolf-man, the fish bones pile high..."

Alasdair hit stop and fast forward. The old man's voice was pleasant and melodic; she wondered if he was the one playing the violin too.

"That's the one about the Wulver," Ewan said with a self-satisfied smile.

Alasdair hit play again.

"When ships first arrived on the island's green shores..."

"This is it!" he said excitedly, and rewound the tape. Blair leaned closer to the tape player as though that might help her analyse what she was about to hear. The first notes of the song sounded different from the others: not a violin but something plucked, like a harp.

"Oh the red deer of Roscoe long protection have known,

From the gods that watch over with hoof and
     with bone.
When ships first arrived on the island's green shores,
 Old Bodach implored them to set down their oars.

Great Guardian Cailleach, protector of the deer,
 Shared not Bodach's hope; the people brought fear,
 Hunting and killing in their sacred domain;
 'They may bring love and caring,' was Bodach's
     refrain.

Cailleach deemed Bodach unfit for his role,
She must take drastic action, no matter its toll.
Knowing no guardian may harm their own kind,
Into a dandelion she transformed a hind.

When Bodach awoke and by hunger was seized,
Sly Cailleach pointed and bade him be eased:
'See how your favourite food grows at your feet?'
Bodach plucked up the dandelion, and the hind he
     did eat.

Cursed was old Bodach, banished from the fey,
'til the new moon brings dark at the end of the day,
And then, in the lightless depths of the loch,
The Fiadh Mho'r, the Sea Stag, sets forth in sleepwalk.

It knows not its name, consumed by its wrath,
It blindly destroys what comes into its path
Cailleach her own cunning magic still weaves,
While Bodach endures his curse without reprieve."

The plucking of the harp gradually ended and there was a moment of crackling silence before the next song began. Alasdair hit stop.

"That's a lot of information," Blair said.

Without replying, Alasdair rewound the tape and played the song again. Blair grabbed her sketchbook, flipped to the back and scribbled down anything important she heard.

C + B protect the deer… People arrived… B likes. C does not

Decides to bump B off?? Transforms HIND? into dandelion

B eats dandelion, cursed.

Hind = deer?

FEE-UGH VORE that EVERYONE keeps talking about.

When the song ended Alasdair glanced at her notes and started laughing. He stole her pen, scribbled out FEE-UGH VORE and replaced it with *Fiadh Mho'r*.

"So-rry, we don't all speak Gaelic," Blair said, taking the pen back.

"A hind is a female deer," Alasdair explained, ignoring

her. "Like a doe. But specific to red deer."

"Right. So Cailleach transformed a deer into a dandelion and tricked Bodach into eating it?"

"Sounds like it."

"That's messed up."

Blair didn't need to meet Alasdair's eyes to know what she would read in his expression. *This* was the person she was doing business with.

"She lied," Blair said, recalling their first conversation. "She told me that Bodach abandoned the fey, that the island was 'out of balance' because of it. But she got rid of him because he wanted to welcome the humans, and she didn't."

"But she *does* want you and your family gone," Alasdair said in a measured tone. "She's not lying about that part."

"Yeah, along with every other human on the island, right? But I basically walked right up to her and offered her an opportunity. Not only am I running errands for her, but she can be rid of my family at the end of it." Blair's jaw clenched, her hands curling into fists. She'd been so stupid.

"Why get my dad involved, though?" Alasdair puzzled.

"Well, she acts like she really cares about all the other fey folk, since she thinks she's the queen of them or something. But I was wondering if she hoped that... that breaking up your family would drive you away," Blair suggested uneasily. "That your heartbroken mum would move you to the mainland or something."

"Maybe," Alasdair said, nodding. "Mum did live on the mainland for a while when she was younger."

Alasdair bit into another scone, brows knitted with concern as he chewed. Blair glanced at her notes again.

"So Bodach became the Fiadh Mho'r? The giant creepy Sea Stag that Morag says is haunting the island. The creature from the stained glass windows..." Blair mused. "Irving told me that if a guardian harms the thing they're supposed to protect, they become cursed."

"And Bodach's curse for eating the hind was to become the Fiadh Mho'r," Alasdair said. "Everyone on Roscoe knows about the Sea Stag. Obviously, I always thought it was just a story. But now..."

"'til the new moon brings dark at the end of the day," Blair recalled. Several things clicked into place at once. "Rosemary said that the Fiadh Mho'r has never harmed anyone – *except* at the new moon."

"*It knows not its name, consumed by its wrath, / It blindly destroys what comes into its path,*" Alasdair recited. "It must not be able to control itself in that form."

Blair slapped her palms onto the table. "And Cailleach said that my next task had to wait until the dark of the moon! It must be something to do with the Fiadh Mho'r!"

Alasdair disappeared up to his room and returned with a book called the *Almanac*. He consulted it briefly. "It's less than a week until the next new moon." His face paled as he met Blair's eyes. "What exactly is she going to expect you to do?"

Several cups of hot chocolate and replays of the song later, Alasdair checked his watch and balked.

"Mum'll be home soon. No offence, but you should probably leave."

"None taken." Blair jumped to her feet and grabbed her backpack; she didn't want to see Aileen any more than the boys' mum probably wanted to see her. Alasdair walked with her to the door, but when she reached for the handle to let herself out, something caught her eye and she paused.

There was a familiar shape in a framed photo beside the door. The yellowing photograph depicted a young girl standing between two smiling parents, and even though it must have been twenty years ago or more, Blair could see at once that the girl was Aileen. Standing proudly behind them all was a ramshackle but beautiful house that Blair would have known anywhere.

"Alasdair," she murmured, not looking away. "Did you know your mum used to live in my house?"

"Oh, um, yeah." He ran a hand through his hair. "It's part of the reason she was a bit... er, salty about you moving here. She always said she was going to buy it back one day."

"You didn't think to mention that?" Blair snapped in disbelief.

"It was already awkward enough!" Alasdair said defensively.

Blair let out a sigh. "That's fair." But she looked closer at the image; there was something weird about it. In the photo, young Aileen was holding a small animal that was reaching up to lick her face. At first Blair thought it was a puppy, but upon closer inspection of its bushy tail and slim snout, she realised it was a fox.

A strange choice for a pet. But that wasn't what made all the blood drain from her face.

The photo was grainy, but she was sure. The colour, the texture, the shape were identical.

Clasped around Aileen's wrist was an antler bracelet.

THE ESCAPE

Blair sat on the garden wall outside her house in the pink glow of dawn, her arms wrapped around her knees. She had come out to check on the owl, but she'd been struck by a sense of unfamiliarity as she seated herself on the cold stone.

The strange feeling grew – the sense that she was in a whole new place. She looked around, soaking it all in. The overgrown meadow that was their front garden had been tidied up, paths mown between the long grass and wildflowers. The outbuildings were freshly painted; the junk that had cluttered the garden was all gone.

When she looked back at the house, she realised that the new coat of whitewash was already finished. The window frames and the front door had been painted sage green, and there were window boxes and hanging baskets overflowing with bright, trailing flowers.

Her parents had done so much while she hadn't even been looking.

She heard a low trill. The owl was standing in the rushes, her bright eyes locked on Blair's.

Blair thought of the fox curled in Aileen's arms in the photo.

She released her legs, sat up straight, and held out one arm. "Come here, little one," she whispered.

For a heartbeat, nothing happened. But then the owl stretched out and flew straight to Blair, her wings beating the air as she settled lightly onto Blair's outstretched forearm. The owl's talons dug into the sleeve of Blair's denim jacket and she winced, her heart racing at the wild creature's proximity.

Blair let out a laugh in shock and the owl took fright and pushed off into the sky. She settled on the edge of the roof.

It took a few minutes for Blair's thundering heart to slow again, and she stayed sitting on the wall, mesmerised by the trust the animal had placed in her.

The front door clicked shut and Blair's mum strolled down the garden path in nothing but her swimming costume; she didn't seem to notice her daughter sitting silently at the edge of the garden. After a moment's contemplation, Blair slipped back into the house to get changed.

When she emerged in her stolen rash vest and shorts, the slight chill on the wind awakened the nerve endings in her legs, her skin erupting in goosepimples. She jogged down the garden and hopped over the wall.

Her mum was standing waist-deep in the water, but she turned back when she heard Blair's footsteps on the turf.

Her face transformed into a wide, bemused smile.

Blair stopped at the water's edge, flinching at the cold tickling her toes. There was barely a ripple in the surface of the aquamarine sea; it looked almost tropical.

"I never thought I'd see the day," her mum remarked.

Blair took one step in, yelped and jumped back out. She folded her arms across her chest and bounced on the balls of her feet. "How do you do this every day?"

"You just have to dive straight in and feel the cold later. Like this. Watch."

Her mum sucked in a breath and dunked herself beneath the surface. She was down for one second, then another, and then she burst up with a gasp, shaking wet tendrils of hair off her face. Blair flinched away from the spray.

"You can't be serious."

But her mum was laughing, sweeping beads of water from her face. "Just don't think about it. Seriously, don't even acknowledge the temperature."

"That makes no sense," Blair said. She took two steps in until she was submerged to her ankles. The cold was biting, and every time it lapped at an untouched area of skin it snapped freshly.

Blair took a deep breath in and sighed it out, walking back onto the sand. As she turned towards the sea again she saw that her mum's face had fallen. But that didn't last long, because Blair let out a scream and propelled herself into the water. Arms wheeling, spray flying from her body, she pushed against the water's resistance until she fell forward and spread out her arms just in time to catch herself. Her strokes were short and quick as she pushed to keep her body moving and her blood flowing.

Her mum clapped, laughing loudly. Between gasps and squeals, Blair realised that the cold was bothering her less and less. Actually, it was kind of exhilarating.

"This is wild," Blair said, switching to a doggy paddle. Her mum sliced through the water in front crawl. Blair swam a bit further out until her toes barely scraped the sand. The sea was so calm it was practically a mirror. She hadn't known the Atlantic could be so still.

Her mum cut a line back towards her and then hovered on the spot, treading water. "Morag said she saw you and Alasdair together yesterday," she said, and there was something a bit uncertain in her tone, as though she was wary of spoiling the moment.

Blair's toes balanced on the sea floor, and she tipped her head back so it was floating on the surface, letting the seawater seep into her hair. "Yep. We fell out for a bit. But it's all good now."

She couldn't see her mum's expression. "We're so glad you're making friends here."

"You never like my friends." The response came automatically.

"That's not true," her mum answered. "It's just hard, being a parent ... seeing your kid go through school. All we want is to know that your friends see you for *you*, not just for your activism – that they see you the way *we* see you. I remember how hard it was when I was a teenager."

"That was a million years ago." Blair was beginning to feel defensive; she didn't want to tread this old ground again.

"It was thirteen years ago, Blair." Something in her mum's voice made Blair raise her head. Her mum's mouth was pinched, her eyes troubled. "I'm only thirty-two. I know that sounds ancient to you, but one day you'll understand it really isn't. I had you straight out of school. Imagine if, six years from now, *you* were pregnant."

Blair's face creased in horror.

"Right?!" To Blair's surprise, her mum laughed. "It's young, okay? We didn't mean to get pregnant, but as soon as I knew, I wanted to have you. But I was worried... about the future. About what was happening in the world we were bringing you into. While you were growing in my belly, I was watching glaciers melting, forests burning on the news." She swallowed, seeming to hesitate over her next words. "I felt very low, all through the pregnancy, and when you were born. That's pretty normal – having a baby is really hard on your body, including your brain. Your dad did his best to look after me, but he was busy working to keep us going."

Blair couldn't look away from her mum's face, even though her gaze was distant, and her eyes were full of tears. She felt like she was seeing, for the first time, not the mum who drove her crazy – but Anna Zielinski.

"Things got so bad that your dad's parents stepped in. They rented a cottage for us, and we used all our savings to go away for a month over summer. We came here, to

Roscoe. The three of us were together every day. We'd cook meals, read books, go for walks, go swimming. Eventually, I was able to think clearly again. I saw the beauty in the world around me, and it gave me hope."

"I didn't know about any of this," Blair muttered.

Her mum smiled wryly. "I never wanted you to think that I was sad about having you. I was unwell. I think you can probably understand that now."

Blair nodded, momentarily lost for words – but then she asked, "If you were worried about the state of the world when I was born... Mum, how come you don't like me protesting?"

"Because I didn't want this to have to be your fight, Blair," Anna answered at once, her voice full of emotion. "I didn't want it to fall to you."

Blair was startled to feel tears pricking at her eyes. "But Mum... this might sound weird, but I'm *glad* to have been born when I was. I'm proud to be a part of everything that's happening. I feel like I'm... ready. Do you know what I mean?"

Her mum swallowed, then nodded. "I want you to know, I never gave up. *This* is how I fight. I remember swimming on our last day here, thinking, what if this wasn't just a temporary fix? What if we could give all of this to Blair? What if we could share this hope with other people? That day we decided that we would save up and come back, and open our B&B. And we did. It just took a bit longer than we expected."

Her mum looked across at her, and suddenly Blair

found she couldn't hold her gaze. She sucked in a breath and ducked beneath the surface, letting her hair float up around her face, opening her eyes to squint into the blue.

What had she done?

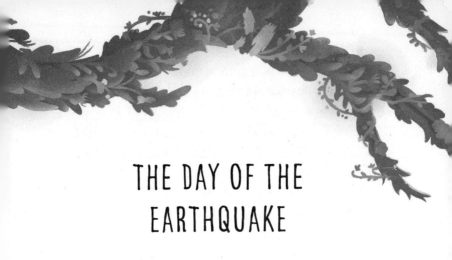

THE DAY OF THE EARTHQUAKE

"There's still so much we don't know," Alasdair said with an edge of frustration.

Blair was sitting by his side on the golden sand at Whalebone Bay, the two of them watching as Sean played with Ewan in the waves. It was another glorious day, but Blair felt like a heavy cloud was hanging over her, a storm brewing. There were only a few days left until the new moon, and Alasdair was right: they'd barely made any progress in their investigation.

"Let's focus on what we *do* know, then," Blair suggested, sitting up straighter. "The third task will have something to do with the Fiadh Mho'r, and somehow, it'll help Cailleach get more humans off the island."

"Bodach has to be a shapeshifter," Alasdair supplied. "I think it's safe to assume that he only takes the form of a giant killer stag during the new moon, because someone probably would have noticed if it had been walking around in daylight all these years."

"Then he could be a cormorant the rest of the time, for all we know. So what are we going to do? Appeal to the Sea Stag's better nature?"

Alasdair's brow flattened as he stared out at the sea. "It doesn't sound like the Fiadh Mho'r has control over its actions."

"No," Blair agreed. "Which means I have to find a way to… outmanoeuvre Cailleach. To do what she says, without her getting what she wants. Otherwise I'm going to be stuck with this hanging around my wrist for ever, and creepy idiots like them following me wherever I go."

She lifted her arm and shook the antler bracelet at the tern, the oystercatcher and the guillemot perched on a nearby boulder, who perked up at the sound.

"That lot are harmless." Alasdair jumped up suddenly and waved his arms, frightening them into flight.

"That lot are the least of my problems," Blair remarked. "You didn't see the bone crabs."

"I'm sorry, the *what*?" Alasdair said. But his watch glinted in the sun, and Blair caught a glimpse of the time.

"Oh! I've got to go. I'm late for crafternoon." She grabbed her backpack and waved to Ewan and Sean before jogging away over the sand.

"We are not done talking about the bone crabs!" Alasdair called after her.

Blair made a quick stop at the general store to buy an envelope and a first-class stamp, then hurriedly stuffed her most recent art project inside. It was scrawled in ballpoint pen, bordered by colour illustrations. An outline of the storm-darkened hills as seen from the ferry was the background to the first page. An illustration of the steading, in all its original ramshackle glory, was at the centre of the next. A herd of Roscoe red deer ambled across the foot of the final page.

Libby had decided to take Blair's silence as a sign that she'd decided to leave her old life and her friends behind. That hurt, but Blair wasn't going to give up that easily. Since picking up the phone was still not an option, she'd explain herself the old-fashioned way.

Blair dropped the envelope into the letterbox outside the shop and crossed the road to Fraoch. The calico cat was lying on the grass in the sunshine. Blair stopped to look at it, and it cracked one eye open to peek at her.

One striking, violet eye.

Blair's breath caught, but in that moment the door opened wide and Morag blinked at her in surprise.

"Hello there, Blair! Here to visit Mother, are you?"

She rolled back to let her in. Blair looked back at the lawn, but the cat had startled at the sound of the opening door, and she could just see its tail disappearing around the side of the house.

As she closed the door behind her, Blair noticed the faded sepia tones of framed family photographs hidden in amongst the images of deer on the walls. After her revelation at the boat house, she wasn't looking past old photos any more. She leaned in close to inspect them, and

Morag noticed her attention.

"She was beautiful as a young woman, wasn't she?"

"This is *Rosemary*?" Blair said in disbelief, gazing on the black-and-white image of a laughing woman in an old-school swimming costume on the beach.

"Oh, yes. She's always loved the water. And look, she used to take me with her." Morag pointed to the next frame along, which depicted Rosemary standing shoulder-deep in the waves, beaming as she supported a small girl. It was undeniably Morag's round face, her legs weightless in the water as her arms fanned out in breaststroke. Blair couldn't help but smile.

"Of course, it's the hills that she loves best. We'd go out as far as we could together – she got me an all-terrain wheelchair, but I've never been as adventurous as Mother. That's why she's always had her solo hikes. She'd leave Father and me playing board games once a month and head off into the hills for hours upon hours." Morag smiled warmly as she waved to the dozens of photos and artworks that made the hallway feel like a gallery. "All of these are hers. Of course, you wouldn't know that – she's never in frame, because she's always the one behind the camera, or wielding the paintbrush."

"I should have known," Blair muttered.

"She and my ex-husband never saw eye to eye. He spent years trying to get permission to build a holiday housing development, but it was always blocked by the Roscoe Biodiversity Trust on the grounds that it would destroy valuable habitat. When he learned that Mother had founded it, that was the last straw. Off he went, back to the mainland, and good riddance!" She chuckled fondly.

Blair's mouth hung open. "Wait. Rosemary *founded* the Trust?"

"Oh, aye. Long time ago. Thanks to her, most of the island is protected for the wildlife – no chance my ex-husband was getting a permit. Anyway, I'd best be off. We've a committee meeting this afternoon."

"Roscoe Needs You? Does that mean Rosemary's busy too?"

"You think there's just the one committee? Oh my child, no. There's the Highland Games Committee; the Creachanns Mountaineering Society; the Sailing Club; the Pensioners' Book Club; the Roscoe Naturalists; the Roscoe Young Naturalists; the Rainbow Seniors Society... I could go on. I'm on most of them! This particular meeting, however, is for the Wild Roscoe Festival Committee. Aileen Reid is the chairwoman, Alasdair's mum, you know. Only a week to go now – it's action stations!"

An idea struck Blair. "Morag, did you know that Aileen Reid used to live in my house?"

Morag didn't look remotely bothered about being delayed. She leaned an elbow on the arm of her chair. "The steading? Aye, her family lived there for generations."

Blair's heart sped up. "So why did they leave?"

"I'm not entirely sure. Speculation was rife, of course. All I know is that it was something to do with the Day of the Earthquake."

Blair straightened, intrigued. "The *what*?"

"The Day of the Earthquake: 24th August 1999, almost exactly twenty-five years ago, now. I remember it well."

"But we're in Scotland! There aren't earthquakes here! Not proper ones..."

Morag spread her hands. "I'm no geologist, but we all felt it. It was around sunset. I was down at the beach with my husband. There was a sound... This otherworldly howl that cut through the sky like lightning. Like the very fabric of the world tearing in two. I'll never forget it." She shuddered.

"Then the whole island trembled. The waves picked up. The sand beneath my wheels was shaking violently. By the time we got to the road, it was over. Still, after a thing like that, you feel like you can never quite trust the ground beneath you." She glanced uneasily at the floor.

Blair shrugged, though her mind was whirring. "Okay, there was an earthquake. But what has that got to do with Aileen?"

Morag clasped her hands in her lap. "Well, it was the steading, you see. Not a crumble nor a crack in any other building on the island, but the steading, somehow, was all but destroyed. The poor family bounced around the village for a while, staying with whoever had the room, but they just couldn't afford the repairs. In the end they went to the mainland."

"That's awful," said Blair uneasily. "But has no one else lived there since? In twenty-five years?"

Morag shook her head. "The Reids sold the place and it changed hands a few times over the years, but no one ever really moved in. Put off by the remoteness of the island or the difficulty of the work to be done. No one was up to the task, until your parents." She smiled, her cheeks dimpling.

"Aileen never tried to buy it back?"

"She talked of little else when she first returned to Roscoe, but she couldn't afford it. And then she met Sean and they built their own house."

Blair's mind was racing: Aileen's antler bracelet, the house destroyed, the Reids forced to leave for the mainland. Cailleach had been involved, and Blair knew in her bones that what the islanders had felt was no ordinary earthquake.

Morag clapped her hands together. "That's enough of a journey down memory lane! I'm off to the meeting, but the door'll lock behind you. Enjoy your crafternoon!"

Blair opened the door for Morag and closed it after her. She glanced up the darkened stairway to the attic; the antler bracelet seemed to weigh heavier on her wrist. Her thoughts were filled with images of the waves rising, the earth shaking, the steading collapsing.

For the first time, she felt like she really understood what was at stake. She needed to think – she needed to plan. Crafternoon was going to have to wait.

"I'm sorry, Rosemary," she murmured. Blair waited until Morag was out of sight and let herself back out of the front door. Then she picked up her bike and cycled away without looking back.

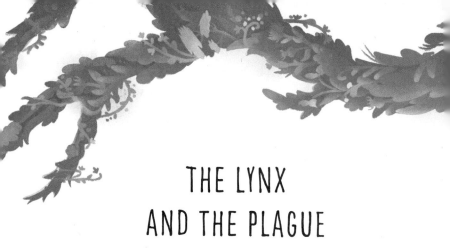

THE LYNX
AND THE PLAGUE

For the next two days Blair's room became mission headquarters as she and Alasdair tried to work out how they could defeat Cailleach. But endless replays of Alasdair's granddad's song didn't reveal any more information, neither of their parents seemed to have any books on local folklore, and the local library turned out to be on wheels – and not due to return to Roscoe for another month. Aileen was working from home, so Alasdair thought it best to keep away from the boat house, but that meant they had no access to the internet. They were still no closer to figuring out a plan.

The whole time, the steading was filled with a constant noise of hammering, hoovering and occasional shouted swear words. But on the morning before the inspection, Blair awoke to a strange quiet. She came upon her parents sitting at the kitchen table with steaming cups of herbata, looking a bit lost.

The welcoming farmhouse kitchen was almost

unrecognisable from the bare, dilapidated room it had been on moving day. The stove was in working order at last and shone where Blair had scrubbed it with an old toothbrush. The cupboards were repaired, the curtains were replaced, every wall was repainted. An assortment of her dad's books about Scottish history and nature were placed on shelves around the room, with herbs hanging to dry between them.

The steading finally felt finished; it felt like somewhere people might actually want to come and stay. It felt like home.

Her dad noticed Blair enter and looked pointedly at her mum. "Kochanie, Blair's here. Didn't you want to…"

"Oh, yes!" Without looking back at Blair, her mum left the room and disappeared up the stairs. Still sleepy, Blair poured herself a glass of orange juice and sat down at the table beside her dad. He blew on his herbata and sipped at it, not saying anything.

Blair's mum returned and, without a word, slid something across the table.

It was her phone. They were giving back her phone!

"I… I thought you'd decided to keep it," Blair stammered as she switched it on.

"I thought about it, but actually I prefer mine," her dad teased.

The screen lit up: fully charged. Blair glanced between her parents and her mum beckoned her out with a nod of her head. "Go on. Give Libby a phone. I'm sure she's missed you."

Blair needed no further encouragement. She shoved her bare feet into her boots and set off out the back door in her tie-dye pyjamas. She was startled by how warm it was today; the sun prickled at her scalp in her parting and warmed her cheeks. It was only the morning, but it already felt like it was going to be the hottest day of the summer.

There was no signal in the back garden, so she climbed over the wall and walked out onto the machair, holding her phone at arm's length. Butterflies floated over the flowers and bees took off from the blooms, loaded up with pollen. Small birds chirped as they dove between the insects and seabirds called high overhead.

Suddenly Blair found a single, wavering bar of signal.

She quickly scrolled to Libby's number and hit dial. Her chest tightened with anxiety as she listened to it ring. Would her friend even pick up after all this time?

"BLAIR!" Libby answered. "She lives! I seriously thought you'd died."

The sound of that warm, familiar tone brought instant tears to Blair's eyes. "Libby!" she cried. She didn't know where to start, so the words came tumbling out together. "I'm really sorry I've been ghosting you – listen – I tried to run away and my parents took my phone and we still don't have internet, everything takes a million years here—"

"Blair, I'm so sorry but I can't talk," Libby interrupted. Blair could hear the sounds of things happening in the background, paint tins rattling and people talking. "We're hanging banners all day to spread the word about the strike. We've got so much ground to cover!"

Blair felt her heart stop. She forced the words out of her dry mouth. "Oh... sorry, I didn't mean to—"

But before she could even finish her thought, Libby was speaking again. "It's so soon now! Can you believe it? I feel like I haven't stopped all summer. People have been messaging me constantly about it. So many people have pledged to join, I think it's going to be huge."

Blair swallowed. "That's so cool—"

Libby cut her off. "You have to convince your parents to let you come back for the day! Anyway, you'll be hearing from me soon. See you later!"

"Seeya," Blair said, but the line was dead. Then she was alone again, fighting off tears.

She had left it too late. She hadn't tried hard enough. She could have asked Alasdair to use his phone. Morag would have let her use Fraoch's computer again if she'd asked. She hadn't been thinking, and now Libby had got used to life without her.

On top of which, *she* had helped get the strikes off the ground, and now they were about to have their biggest ever event *without* her.

It was too much. She clutched the phone to her chest, her mind reeling.

"Tonight is the night," said a voice behind Blair, and her heart sank even lower.

When Blair turned, she found Cailleach standing in the machair, her toes curled into the sandy soil, the sun glinting behind her antlers. They were no more than a hundred metres from the steading; Cailleach had never been this near to her home before. Blair felt a low current of unease as she thought of her parents so close at hand.

The tune of the ballad unfurled in Blair's mind, reminding her of everything she had learned since she last saw this wild guardian of the deer. The last time, she'd been running. But not today.

"What's my task?" she asked, her voice steady.

Discontent flashed over Cailleach's face, though it was quickly smoothed away. Blair knew that her composure had thrown the guardian.

"After all our work together, that is all you have to say? Suit yourself." Cailleach looked Blair up and down. "Do well, and you will be on the first ferry home in the morning."

Blair thought of the strike, of Libby, the mainland. She sucked in her bottom lip. She said nothing.

"Fail, Blair Zielinski, and you will never be free." Cailleach's voice rumbled low like thunder.

Blair felt the weight of the antler bracelet on her wrist, its uncanny coldness. The sun beat down on her skin, sweat prickling along her arms, but the bone was cool.

"Tonight, at last, is the dark of the moon," Cailleach went on. "Your task is simple: find the brùnaidh of this house and bring it to the sea loch when the sun reaches the hills."

Sunset at the new moon. Their suspicions were right: somehow, the Fiadh Mho'r was involved in all this.

As always, the instructions were cryptic and incomplete, but for once, Cailleach was still standing there. "What is it that you want me to bring?" Blair asked. "A brownie?"

Cailleach's eyes narrowed. *"Brùnaidh,"* she repeated.

It sounded a lot like 'brownie' to Blair's ears. She had less than a day to figure out what it actually was, to find the one that belonged to her house and bring it to Cailleach. What happened after that was shrouded in mystery.

Strangely enough, Cailleach hovered there a moment longer, as if finally giving Blair the chance to ask the follow-up questions she usually ignored. Blair met Cailleach's burning eyes briefly; there was something there she hadn't seen before, something uncertain.

But Blair wouldn't trust Cailleach's words, even if she answered.

For the first time, Blair turned her back on the guardian and walked away.

As soon as Blair had closed the door behind her, she paused to take a moment. She had barely breathed as she walked away from the guardian who had sent her fleeing from ghost-crows and the howls of werewolves. But at least Cailleach had seemed unsure of herself: that gave her hope.

The only trouble was, now she had to figure out what to do.

"Brùnaidh, brùnaidh…" she muttered to herself under her breath. She retreated to her bedroom and pulled out the big pieces of paper she and Alasdair had been using to map out their ideas and findings over the past couple of days.

She needed to go over everything she knew and figure out her plan. She needed Alasdair.

The first question, however – what exactly *was* a brùnaidh?

Suddenly remembering the gift she had received only ten minutes earlier, Blair pulled her phone out of her pocket and opened the browser. But the faint trace of signal she had chanced upon was long gone, and the phone obstinately insisted on No service.

She scanned their scribbled notes, but she knew in her heart that it was fruitless. She was certain she'd never heard the word before today.

"Are you planning to spend the day in your pyjamas?"

Blair jumped. Her dad smiled from the doorway.

"I haven't had time to get changed yet. I'm planning, um, a craft project with Rosemary."

Her dad's face brightened; he didn't seem to have noticed the obvious lie. "What was that word you were muttering?"

Blair was willing to try anything at this point. "Do you know what a brùnaidh is?"

"A brownie?" her dad questioned. "Brownie, chocolate or brownie, fairy?"

Blair laughed, confused, but her dad looked serious. "Brownie, fairy?" she suggested.

Her dad walked into the room and sat down on the edge of her bed. "Like in the story I used to tell you when you were small. *The Lynx and the Plague*. Remember?"

It rang the tiniest of bells in her mind, but Blair shook her head.

"Really? It was your favourite when you were four."

Blair rolled her eyes.

"Really, it was. My tata told it to me in Polish when I was small, but I translated it to English for you. A brownie is a magical creature that lives in your house – like a household fairy. The stories say that wherever people make a home, a brownie is born. It takes the shape of an animal and watches over the home and the people who live there."

Blair's breath caught in her throat. "Do you still remember the story?"

Her dad looked up into the corner of the room, plumbing the depths of his memory. "Yes, I think I do."

Without another word Blair sat up and crossed her legs, turning to face him. Her dad laughed nervously, as though unsure what to do with his daughter's rapt attention. But then he looked past her to the window and began to speak.

"There was once a peasant who had been away from home for a long time, working. Maybe she was a fisherwoman, I'm not sure exactly. When her work was finished she began the long journey home, and every day she walked from dawn until dusk. One afternoon, when she was sitting under a tree eating her lunch, a woman approached her. She was old, all skin and bones with long, grey hair. But she had a friendly face.

"The peasant stood up to greet her out of respect for her elders and the old woman put her arms around her at once and embraced her. The gesture was warm, but she was cold as the grave. The old woman said to her, 'I am the Plague. Now you must carry me upon your shoulders wherever you go.'

"The peasant found she had no choice in the matter; the woman was on her shoulders and there would be no removing

her. Still, she had to get home, so she continued on her way. But she was horrified to find that in every village she passed through, everyone around her fell down dead.

"The peasant was almost home, where her partner raised their three children, and the agony of what would soon come to pass was tearing her apart. She knew that if her family opened the door to her, they would all be doomed. But the peasant had grown up in that house with her own parents, and she knew the place inside and out. An idea came to her.

"As she climbed the hill to her home with the Plague on her shoulders, she called out to her family, 'Do not open the door! I am home, but you must not greet me.' Then she shouted again, 'Lynx! Come out.' For as long as her family had lived in this house, the lynx, their brownie, had been bound to it. It had been protecting the home and its inhabitants all her life.

"Now, the great spotted cat with its tufted ears prowled around to the front of the house. When it saw the Plague sitting atop the peasant's shoulders, it snarled and growled and made ready to pounce. The old woman, frightened, instantly let go of the peasant and ran away.

"Having protected the family, the lynx slunk away to its den, for it was a wild creature and not a pet. The peasant was reunited with her family, and the Plague never visited their home."

Blair was awash with emotions she could hardly name. The memories the story had dredged up were so vivid: lying in her warm bed, the way the mattress sank to accommodate her dad's weight when he sat beside her. The timbre of his voice was the same. How she used to picture her mum in the role of the young fisherwoman, the old woman clinging to her shoulders. It had all been there, buried; the lynx imagined as a fluffy cat with big fangs, before she had known what one looked like.

The lynx that was part of the peasant woman's home. An animal that shared its soul.

Blair thought back to the black-headed gull that always seemed to be perched on the roof of Alasdair's boat house. The calico cat that prowled the flowerbeds of the Fraoch Guest House. The photo of Aileen outside the steading with the fox in her arms.

The photo had been small and yellowed, but Blair would have bet her life that the fox's eyes were as violet as the gull's, and the cat's – and her owl's.

She had just jumped to her feet when the door burst open and her mum strode into the room. "There you both are! Józef, I need someone to stir the onions for the bigos."

Blair's dad stood up and saluted. "Reporting for duty, chef. I promised the committee the finest Polish meal they'd ever eaten."

"I need to go into the village to see Alasdair," Blair said hurriedly. "Are you going to need my help?"

Blair's mum seemed momentarily taken aback that her daughter had offered at all. "We'll be just fine, Blair. Haven't you heard the saying 'too many cooks'?"

"Great. Good luck!" Blair pushed them both towards the door and closed it behind them.

It was probably the fastest clothes change she had ever accomplished. As she hopped out into the front garden,

229

pulling on one shoe, Blair scanned the house for some sign of the owl – but the nest seemed unoccupied, and she wasn't perched on the roof either.

She must be out hunting. Blair grabbed her bike from the outbuildings, and in the next minute she was racing down the road, unbrushed hair flying out behind her, her untied shoelaces flapping in the wind.

A BROKEN BRACELET

It was Alasdair who answered the knock on the boat house's front door, and his face lit up as soon as he saw Blair on his doorstep. "I've been waiting to hear from you all morning. Tonight's the new moon!"

Blair was too distracted to respond. "Is your mum home?"

That wiped the smile from his face. "She's upstairs. What's going on?"

He ushered her in, and Blair pointed to the photo in the hallway. Alasdair peered at it.

"Yeah, Mum used to live in your house. We've been over this already."

"But look at this." Blair jabbed a finger at young Aileen, leaving a fingerprint on the dusty glass. "She has a bracelet just like mine. Just like the one Cailleach stuck me with." She touched the bracelet on her wrist. It was too hot for long sleeves today, so it was plain for all to see.

Alasdair squinted and moved closer to the frame. His

lips parted as realisation dawned. "Mum made a deal with Cailleach too."

"And the house she lived in was destroyed. *My* house. On the Day of the Earthquake, twenty-five years ago."

"She refuses to talk about that day," Alasdair breathed.

"*And* Cailleach appeared this morning and told me to bring the brùnaidh of my house to the sea loch tonight."

"Your house spirit! I – why am I still surprised by any of this?" Alasdair said, stopping himself short. "But... do you know what it is? Where to find it?"

"I think so." Blair pointed to the animal in young Aileen's arms. "I think this fox was your mum's."

Alasdair's brows rose. "I always assumed it was a dog..."

"Did I hear the door?" a voice called down from above, and there were footsteps on the stairs.

Aileen stopped in her tracks when she saw Blair. Her jaw clenched.

"Mum, please don't be weird," Alasdair said quickly.

But Aileen raised a finger and levelled it at Blair. "*That girl* is not welcome in this house."

Alasdair shifted his weight so that he was between his mum and Blair. "Mum, listen to me. I already told you she didn't realise what would happen. She thought she was doing the right thing. You've got to work it out with Dad now. It's not Blair's fault."

Aileen folded her arms tightly across her chest, not meeting her son's eyes. "I don't understand how she even *knew* to get involved—"

Blair cut across her, holding up her right arm. "Does

this answer your question?"

Aileen looked at the antler bracelet and her face paled. She reached out to clutch the banister for support. "Cailleach," she whispered.

The name hung in the air between them. Alasdair was agog, but his mum recovered herself, pinching her nose to rub the corners of her eyes. When she spoke again, her voice was measured. "I think we could all use a cup of tea."

Blair and Alasdair sat in the galley kitchen, two mugs of tea steaming in front of them. Floorboards creaked upstairs, and then there were footsteps on the stairwell, and a moment later Aileen returned to the room.

She set something down in front of them. It was in two pieces: a round, textured object, white as bone.

An antler bracelet.

"You made a deal with Cailleach?" Alasdair said, his voice pained.

Aileen sat down opposite them, scooping her mug into her hands and staring into it. "It was the biggest mistake I ever made."

"What happened on the Day of the Earthquake?" Blair asked.

"They told me Cailleach wasn't real," Aileen murmured. "That she was a figment of my imagination. No one believed me when I told them the truth."

Alasdair reached out to lay a hand over his mum's. "I believe you, Mum," he said gently.

Aileen met his eyes with the trace of a smile. She took a deep breath in. "I hated life on Roscoe. I was a teenager and I was bored out of my mind. I made a wish out loud. It was answered."

Blair felt the hairs on the back of her neck stand up.

"Cailleach told me that if I helped her, I could go to the mainland, far away, and I'd never have to come back. But she wanted Twig – *my* Twig. The fox who lived in the garden. I'd grown up with him, and he was the most gentle creature in the world…"

There were tears in her eyes, and she flicked them away.

"I didn't want to bring him to her. But she told me it was too late. If I didn't do as she said, she'd set the creature on *us* instead, my family…"

"What creature?" Blair asked.

A crease appeared between Aileen's brows. "The Cù-Sìth."

"Thrice barks the Cù-Sìth, and leaps on a-hunting…" Alasdair recited. "From Granddad's songs."

"It's gone now," Aileen said stonily. "She wanted it gone for good. It had been preying on her deer."

Blair remembered the hound Alasdair had told her about when they'd first started looking for the kelpie, whose three barks spelled doom. If it was anything like the wildcat they'd encountered, or the crodh mara she'd met on the beach, then it was just a dog – a magical dog, true. But like the kelpie, surely it had only been hunting the deer to eat, to survive? Had it deserved to attract the wrath of their protector?

"I brought Twig to her, but I didn't realise what she would do… She transformed him… Turned him into something else. A hare. She set him outside the lair of the Cù-Sìth. That thing – it snatched up Twig in its jaws—" she half-sobbed – "and a moment later, it was like… the Cù-Sìth folded in on itself. And dissolved. Like a thousand dandelion seeds on the breeze, until it was nothing."

Aileen followed the seeds in her mind's eye with her gaze, and Blair found herself staring after them too. Her heart was racing.

Irving's words stirred in her mind: *No fey creature can harm another. That's a sure-fire way to land a curse on your head.* "She used the brùnaidh to curse the Cù-Sìth," Blair said. "She had to disguise the brùnaidh so the Cù-Sìth wouldn't know it was another fey creature."

"Her signature move," Alasdair muttered under his breath.

"The sound was like nothing else I've ever heard," Aileen went on. "Like the screech of a hundred wolves howling. And then the earth shook. Our home collapsed. It was a miracle my parents survived…"

Tears were running freely down her face now. "We had to leave the island, go to the mainland, just as she said we would. But my parents hated the city, and so did I."

Alasdair pushed out his chair and moved around the table to his mum's side. He put an arm around her. "But Mum, you came back," he said gently. "You met Dad, and you had us… You built our house."

Aileen pressed a hand to her mouth, squeezing her eyes

shut. "I don't know who I am without Sean," she said, muffled and quiet. "Why would he ever come back after what I've done?"

Blair looked across at Alasdair, feeling out of her depth. He didn't seem to know what to do either. Blair remembered how shaken she'd felt when she'd seen the tears on her mum's cheeks after their argument.

"I'd better go," she said, leaving her tea untouched on the table. But Aileen reached suddenly across to clasp her wrist just above the antler bracelet.

"Don't make the same mistake I did," Aileen said fervently. "Don't let her destroy what your parents have built. I've been over the events of that day a thousand times, trying to work out how I could have saved Twig and the house."

She relinquished her hold, but her eyes never left Blair's.

"*Listen* to what Cailleach says. Take her at her word."

Blair had just taken her first step away from the house when the door opened again behind her, and Alasdair stepped out onto the garden path.

"Dad told me he wants to talk to Mum," he said, just low enough that he wouldn't be overheard from indoors. "I'm going to take her to the bay to see him. But I'll be there with you tonight, Blair. I promise."

Blair felt warmth spreading from her chest out to her fingertips, despite the anxious cloud in her mind. "Cailleach said to meet her at the sea loch when the sun reaches the hills."

"You know what it means, don't you?"

Blair nodded. "She wants to pull the same trick she did on the Cù-Sìth twenty-five years ago. First she tricked Bodach into harming the thing he was meant to protect and cursed him to become the Fiadh Mho'r. Now she's decided to destroy the Fiadh Mho'r for good by having it kill another fey creature... *my* brùnaidh."

"You won't be facing her alone," Alasdair said. Blair threw her arms around him and squeezed him tight.

When they separated, he placed something into her hand. It was his mum's broken bracelet. "Would you do me a favour and get rid of this thing?"

"Of course." Blair closed her hand around it.

"I'll see you at the sea loch," he said, and disappeared inside.

Blair looked up at the violet-eyed gull that had been watching their exchange from the chimney stack. "I'll keep him safe," she told it.

She walked up the road until she came to the bridge over the river, then she followed the path down the bank until she was out of earshot of the houses. She sat at the water's edge, turning the pieces over in her hands.

"I seriously hope you're not thinking of littering," Irving said.

Blair lifted her head to find the river guardian sitting on the opposite bank, feet dangling in the water.

"You're going to dry out if you stay out here. I'm roasting," Blair warned them.

But Irving was focused on Blair's hands. "What have you got?" they asked.

Blair shrugged. "Just some broken bracelet."

When she looked up, she saw that Irving's eyebrows were raised. "Believe it or not, I wasn't born yesterday," they said. "I may look about twelve, but I'm as old as this river, which makes me just as old as *she* is." This was said with a pointed nod to the two bracelets: one broken, one whole.

"It'll all be over by the end of the day, one way or another," Blair said. "I think I know what I need to do."

Irving folded one leg and drew it in to their chest, wrapping their arms around it. "Let me tell you something about Cailleach," they said. "She's the guardian of the deer just like I am for this river, just like there's one for every kind of tree and flower and insect. But some time long ago she got it into her head that the deer are the most important thing on this island, and that's where she's wrong. Every beetle, every shrub, every scallop is just as important to Roscoe as her deer. Every single living thing belongs on this island. Get it?"

It was the longest speech Blair had ever heard them make, and she was slightly taken aback. Blair chewed on her bottom lip.

"Even humans?" she finally asked. "Even when we build over habitats and fill the oceans with plastic?"

Irving's eyes were filled with sorrow when they met Blair's. "Even humans," they said meaningfully. "It's true – some humans do those things. Some humans think like

Cailleach, that they're more important than everything else. But that's their mistake, and it isn't your fault. *You* belong here. We *all* belong here. We will figure it out. We will make it right."

Blair felt tears threatening and looked down at her clasped hands. Irving sighed.

"Right then. I officially give you permission to litter. It's organic material anyway," they said airily.

Blair felt the shards of bone clack together in her palm as she held out her hand. Then she tossed the broken pieces of Aileen's bracelet into the river. They sank beneath the surface, and the current swept them away.

By the time Blair got home, the sun was high in the sky and her T-shirt was damp with sweat. She approached the reeds at the side of the house. A few feet from the nest she crouched down, and a pair of violet eyes bobbed up to meet hers. She tentatively extended her hand and whistled.

Without a second's hesitation, the owl hopped out of the grass and crossed the ground towards her. The next thing she knew, the bird was perched on Blair's forearm, ruffling her feathers. She had finally lost the last of her fledgling fluff; her feathers were sleek and glossy. Her beak was curved and sharp, and a little moss from her nest clung to her huge claws.

She was fully grown. She had grown with their house.

"Moss," Blair said. "That's what we'll call you."

The owl looked at her quizzically, and Blair laughed. But she felt her joy waver in the face of what lay ahead.

Cailleach had sacrificed a brùnaidh to destroy another fey creature and drive the Reids from the island in one fell swoop. And now she wanted to do the same to *her* brùnaidh. *Her* family.

Her home.

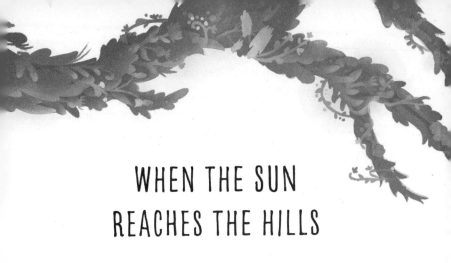

WHEN THE SUN
REACHES THE HILLS

When Blair let herself into the house, the kitchen was warm and brimming with the delicious smells of stewing vegetables and sauerkraut. A loaf of freshly baked bread sat on a cooling rack beside the stove, where her mum was stirring the pot while her dad rinsed mushrooms in the sink.

Despite the fact that her mum didn't speak any Polish, they were both singing loudly to a Polish song on the radio. They mustn't have heard her come in.

Blair smiled in bemusement and walked up between them. Both of them jumped. She reached for the bread, but her mum rapped her knuckles with the handle of the wooden spoon. "I *don't* think so! This is all for tomorrow."

In response, Blair threw open the fridge door and stuffed a cold mushroom pie into her mouth – she was going to need all her strength. She shrugged into her torn waterproof and tucked the map she'd made of the island into her pocket, checking it before she rolled it away: the sea loch was on the north-eastern coast of the island, an area she'd missed out when she was searching the coast for seals. She'd only ever seen it shining from the distance when she'd been high in the hills. If she was going to make it by sunset, she needed to leave now.

"Where do you think you're going?" her mum asked.

Blair flinched, pausing with her hand on the door handle. "I'm just going for a walk with Alasdair."

"Hold on," her dad said firmly, and Blair turned around. "The inspection is tomorrow, Blair. We've let you have your freedom all summer, but we need your help tonight."

"There are still a hundred things to do before the committee arrives," her mum agreed. "Send Alasdair a message and tell him you can't make it."

Blair felt her chest tighten. Her parents were right: they had barely asked her to lift a finger all summer, and now, after the peace offering of the phone, all they wanted her to do was stay in for one evening.

They were both watching her, waiting. The cautious look in their eyes was the most painful thing of all, because they were *expecting* her to defy them.

And she had to.

"No," she said, trying to inject some venom into her voice. "I can't. I promised him." She heard her voice wavering, saw her dad beginning to shake his head. She needed to make it convincing, so she forced herself to add: "I don't *want* to help you pass the inspection so we can be stuck here for ever."

Before they could respond, she darted through the

door, letting it slam behind her. She waited a moment, heart racing, on the other side. Neither of them followed.

Blair pushed down the wave of guilt and shame that threatened to submerge her. She took a deep breath.

Outside, the house cast a long shadow over the garden. The sun was slowly descending, but not yet within reach of the hills.

When she rounded the house, Moss was not in her nest. Blair felt a brief flash of panic before reasoning that she couldn't be far away. She whistled, long and loud.

She never heard a sound, but suddenly Moss was soaring down from the sky towards her, and Blair threw up her arm for the bird to land on. The owl's talons dug into Blair's bare skin and she winced.

"Follow me," Blair said, and raised her arm again. Moss beat her wings and lifted back into the sky.

Her body humming with adrenaline, Blair set off running into the hills.

The miserable moment with her parents faded from her mind at the wondrous sight of the owl following her path from the air.

There was a distant, shrill whinny, and in the next moment, the kelpie-horse came cantering over the machair towards her. Blair slowed to catch her breath as the horse trotted in a circle around her.

"I'm not sure you want to go where we're going," Blair said between breaths. "She's not the biggest fan of yours."

The kelpie-horse only snorted, picking up his hooves in long strides that ate up the ground in Blair's wake.

So, in the shadow of an owl and with a horse on her heels, Blair made her way to the sea loch.

Waves lapped at the shore. Peat bog became pebbles where dark water crept around reed beds. The Atlantic rushed into the long loch through a narrow inlet in the rock wall, like a chink in the island's armour, a gateway between land and sea. A place on the edge of two worlds, seawater locked into land. The sun was only now beginning to tease at the ridges of the hills.

Blair's heart was racing and her ears felt hypersensitive to the calling of oystercatchers, the wind in the reeds, the kelpie-horse's snorts. Moss flew in wide circles overhead. Blair felt a shiver of fear as she looked up at the beautiful creature that had put its trust in her.

There was movement at the water's edge, and Blair's eyes were drawn to a figure further along the shore, turning over an old rowing boat. It wasn't Cailleach, that much was certain. Blair walked towards them with the kelpie-horse at her shoulder.

Clad in navy blue overalls, Rosemary glanced at Blair as she pushed the rowing boat out into the loch. Water sloshed around her ankles, protected by a pair of wellington boots.

Her sharp eyes found the brùnaidh in the sky.

"I thought I might be seeing you, Blair Zielinski," Rosemary said, her voice betraying nothing.

Blair was speechless. Her hand found the antler bracelet

at her wrist and she clasped it tightly, not knowing how to begin to explain.

"You be careful, lass," Rosemary warned as she stepped into the boat. She sat down heavily and picked up the oars, sliding them beneath the water's surface and pushing herself out with the ease of a woman half her age. "This is no place for fey nor human creatures once the sun sets. Get yourself home."

"What about you?" Blair called after her.

A small smile lit Rosemary's face; Blair could see it even across the ever-increasing distance between them. "Don't you worry about me."

Far out, above deep, heaving water, the old woman stopped rowing. The boat rocked as she got to her feet.

Rosemary met Blair's eyes. Without another word, she stepped over the edge of the boat and dropped into the water.

"Rosemary!" Blair cried, but the rolling waves remained unbroken. She was gone.

"Blair!" called a familiar voice, and Blair turned, heart hammering, to see Alasdair running towards her. He dropped his hands to his knees to catch his breath when he reached her, puffing out, "Was that – Rosemary Duncan?"

"*Alasdair!* You're here! Rosemary just stepped off the boat – I think that means—"

"Rosemary can take care of herself," a cold voice said from behind them.

Apprehension dropped like a stone in Blair's stomach as she turned to face Cailleach.

The wind picked up, whipping at Cailleach's hair and clothing. Her eyes were set in hard determination. She looked more fey, less human, than she ever had. Her gaze flickered over Alasdair, who was standing rigid at Blair's side.

"Your mother was never supposed to return," Cailleach said darkly.

"Sucks to be you, I guess," Alasdair shot back. Blair bit back a grin. She was so relieved that Alasdair was here beside her, that she didn't have to face Cailleach alone.

Cailleach turned her face away from him. "Where is the brùnaidh?" she demanded.

Blair looked up at the owl in the sky; she was high enough that the last rays of sunlight caught her underbelly, painting her the colour of smouldering embers. Blair held up her arm and whistled.

Moss changed course and soared down towards her, and Blair braced herself as the owl landed on her arm. She beat her wings once more before tucking them away.

"You have done well," Cailleach said with guarded approval. "Now give it to me."

Listen to what Cailleach says, Aileen had told her. *Take her at her word.*

Blair took a step backwards, drawing the owl close to her body. "No."

Cailleach's face darkened.

"I'm not giving you anything," Blair continued, faltering only slightly. "You said that my task was to bring the brùnaidh to the sea loch at sunset. I've done that. We're here. I've kept my end of the bargain."

It was a gamble, and if she was wrong, Blair didn't know what she'd do. But Cailleach's eyes burned, and in the next moment, the bracelet of bone on Blair's wrist cracked. She felt it splinter, and glanced down in alarm just as the antler tumbled free and fell to the ground in pieces.

Blair's gaze shot up to Cailleach, a smile lighting her face, vindicated.

She was right. The bargain was done.

Cailleach's eyes were ablaze, and her voice rose in pitch. "This is *not* a negotiation."

There was a shudder underfoot. Blair's eyes flicked to the loch. Out in the centre where the rowing boat drifted, the surface of the water was agitated, rippling.

"I won't make you hold up your end," Blair said, finding Cailleach's eyes again. She forced a steeliness into her voice, though her whole body was rushing with adrenaline. "Just let us go."

Cailleach was shaking her head before Blair had even finished speaking. "You are a small piece in this puzzle, Blair Zielinski. Much greater things are in motion. Tonight, the Fiadh Mho'r will kill a fey creature, and be gone at last from this world. Tonight, I will finally be rid of Bodach once and for all."

In that very moment, the last of the sunlight vanished behind the hills with a flash of rose-pink.

In the twilight, the surface of the sea loch erupted. Like an island emerging from beneath the depths, a hulking mass heaved itself slowly from the loch floor. Dark as the depths, its antlers draped with seaweed, a colossal stag was taking form.

Blair felt the water of the loch brimming out and lapping at her feet, but she stood her ground.

"I won't give her to you!"

"Foolish child," Cailleach growled. "The boy's mother tried to back out too, but I made sure her wish came true. Clearly I was not thorough enough! This time that house will crumble!"

She lunged towards the owl in a sudden rush of motion. Blair flinched away and Moss took flight, flapping up and up into the sky.

The water of the sea loch was flooding out, rushing across the peat, soaking them to their knees. The kelpie-horse was snorting, his nostrils flaring, leaning back against the pressure of the water.

The creature in the loch broke free of the surface. Waterfalls cascaded from the back of the Fiadh Mho'r.

Blair's heart thundered. She had to break Bodach's curse. To save Moss, to protect the house. The house where her parents were right at this moment, with no idea of the danger they were in.

"Blair, we need to move." Alasdair grabbed Blair by the arm and tugged her away. They pushed through the water together towards an outcrop of rock at the loch's edge, and Alasdair scrambled up, hauling Blair after him. The kelpie-horse waited at the foot of the crag, his trembling legs submerged to the knees.

As soon as they were both above the waterline Blair grabbed Alasdair by the shoulders. "Do you remember the song about Cailleach and Bodach? The last verse?"

Alasdair panted, his eyes darting as he racked his brains. "It's – something like – *It knows not its name, consumed by its wrath, / It blindly destroys*—"

"It doesn't know its name," Blair breathed.

Alasdair's eyes widened in dawning comprehension. "It doesn't remember it's Bodach. But maybe if we remind it—"

"—we can break the curse!" Blair finished for him.

The Fiadh Mho'r was taking shape before them. Each cloven hoof was the size of a boulder, its legs longer than the tallest pines on the island. Its eyes, black as a moonless night, took in its surroundings without recognition.

Moss had flown right into its path. The creature's head turned, its eyes locking on the owl beating her wings in front of its face.

The great deer inhaled, long and deep, and let out an unearthly bellow that reverberated around the hills.

Cailleach was still standing on what had been the shore of the loch, water swirling around her to the waist. Unmoving, she watched the giant deer with hungry eyes.

The Fiadh Mho'r took its first step towards the owl. Moss spun and flew fast away from the creature, but in one lumbering stride that shook the ground below, the stag closed the distance between them again.

"Bodach!" Blair shouted at the top of her lungs.

"BODACH!" Alasdair joined in.

"*BODACH!*" they called together.

But it had no effect.

The Fiadh Mho'r snapped at the owl with its teeth, narrowly missing. The kelpie-horse whinnied and barrelled towards them in a flat-out gallop. Blair's jaw dropped as the brave horse darted around the Sea Stag's legs. The Fiadh Mho'r stumbled, falling to one knee, buying them a moment of time.

Blair's mind raced. Reminding it of its name wasn't working.

But the creature wasn't Bodach any more. No longer a guardian, like Cailleach.

Cursed was old Bodach, banished from the fey...

So *who* had Bodach become?

"Bodach!" Alasdair yelled again beside her, waving his arms over his head, still trying to catch the creature's attention.

As she stared at her friend, Alasdair's words rang in Blair's ears. *I'd found my true name. The one I was meant to have.*

"Stop!" Blair cried, and Alasdair turned to her, alarmed. "It's the wrong name," Blair said urgently. "We got it wrong!"

The empty rowing boat was still rocking on the disturbed waters of the loch. The rowing boat that Rosemary had stepped out of, plunging into the water without a trace of fear.

Rosemary, who had taken every photo, painted every image of the deer that covered the walls of Fraoch.

250

Rosemary, who hadn't fully trusted Blair since she'd seen the antler bracelet on her wrist. Rosemary – who had founded the Roscoe Biodiversity Trust, who had fought to protect the island's wildness.

Bodach wasn't the Fiadh Mho'r's true name any more.

Blair grabbed Alasdair's sleeve. "You said it yourself – Bodach must be a shapeshifter. At the new moon, they have to transform into the Fiadh Mho'r. But what about the rest of the time? Bodach can't have looked the same all these years, because someone would have noticed, right? I bet that Bodach can take whatever form fits them best. And they've had a long, long time to learn who they really are."

What was the true essence of the Fiadh Mho'r? The ancient guardian of the deer, or the flint-eyed, crafty old woman who watched all the island's comings and goings from her attic workshop?

Alasdair's brow furrowed, and he opened his mouth to speak, but the giant stag was heaving itself to its feet. Moss screeched and the Fiadh Mho'r swung its head, its antlers slicing through the air, just out of reach of the owl. The terrified brùnaidh was heading for home, leading the Fiadh Mho'r with her, and the loch water racing around its hooves was flooding the valley.

Blair's breath was coming fast. She needed to act, *now*. She punched her fist into the air and held it there. "Come back!" she called to the owl.

Moss banked and turned.

The Fiadh Mho'r was a moment delayed. It heaved its

great body around and set off in pursuit of the owl that was now slicing through the darkening sky towards Blair. The kelpie-horse wove in and out of its legs, but he was an insect to the enormous stag, whose lumbering steps barely registered his presence.

Blair's chest heaved, her arm ached, but she held fast until the owl collided with her, grasping onto her arm. The Fiadh Mho'r was a few strides away, looming over them like a mountain, a tidal wave of seaweed and brine. Alasdair grabbed onto her other arm.

"I know your name!" Blair shouted as another massive step shook the earth. "Your name is ROSEMARY DUNCAN!"

The creature's step faltered. It skidded to a halt, sending a shower of peat and soil over them. The stag roared. It was a sound that made the very earth tremble, and afterwards the great deer held its head high, the whites of its eyes flashing.

Then the hiss of rushing water became a cacophony, and Blair ducked as the creature dissolved in a cascade of brackish water. The owl took flight just as Blair and Alasdair were knocked to the ground by the surge. Blair gripped Alasdair's hand and held tight until the downpour subsided, though her glasses were washed from her face.

The rushing sound began to fade, and when Blair opened her eyes again in the near-darkness she could just make out the briny water draining back into the loch.

Close at hand, she heard the beating of wings and the full-body shudder of the horse shaking water from its coat.

Alasdair was groaning as he pushed himself back to his feet. Blair felt around the ground for the hard frame of her glasses, but she couldn't find them. How could she face Cailleach if she couldn't see her?

"I think these are yours, spy," said a friendly voice. Blair took the item that was being proffered to her and pulled the frames onto her face with relief. Though the lenses were spotted with droplets, she could make sense of the world at last. And smiling down at her, overalls heavy with water, was Rosemary.

WITH FLYING COLOURS

Only the faintest line of light on the horizon gave them anything to see by. Blair gave Alasdair a hand to pull him to his feet, then turned at once to her animals. Moss was perched on the highest point of the crag, preening her damp feathers and looking rather disgruntled. The kelpie-horse was scratching at his shoulder with his teeth, giving off a noticeable smell of wet dog. Blair smiled in relief.

But when she looked down from their outcrop and saw Cailleach, motionless as a standing stone on the shore of the loch, her face fell.

Blair left Alasdair and Rosemary behind and scrambled down the crag. She squelched determinedly through the trenches of the Fiadh Mho'r's hoofprints until she was face to face with Cailleach once again. The guardian's mouth was a thin line.

"We're done now," Blair said, giving her voice an edge of iron. "Leave my family alone. I won't let you manipulate me any more."

Cailleach narrowed her eyes and tutted. "Changeable humans. One can never put any trust in your word."

Blair heard a deep sigh at her side and realised that Rosemary and Alasdair had come up behind her.

"After all this time, Cailleach?" Rosemary said, in a voice Blair hadn't heard her use before: commanding, weary. "I've spent every new moon lumbering around the island out of my senses for the past ten thousand years. Yet *now* you decide to put an end to me?"

"You were banished from the fey, Bodach," Cailleach snapped. "You are no longer a guardian. But you are still interfering in the lives of *my* deer – treating them as though they are no more important than any other living thing on this island!"

Rosemary rolled her eyes. "That old refrain? I may not be a guardian any more, but I've done everything I can to keep Roscoe wild, for *all* of us."

Cailleach's face clouded. "The girl called upon your true essence. You are human through and through now. Is that really the choice you would make?"

"Not much of a choice!" Rosemary scoffed. "If you'd had it your way I'd have been snuffed out like a candle! No, thank you – I'd much rather be my own woman amongst friends."

"Condemned to a human's mortality!" Cailleach retorted. "How will you protect the deer when you are cold in the ground?"

Rosemary let out a laugh. "You've made it quite clear that you don't think me capable of protecting them." She laid one hand firmly on Blair's shoulder and the other on Alasdair's. "But I have faith in the next generation."

"Humans will be the death of us all if left unchecked," Cailleach said coldly. "I will see to it that every last one of them leaves this place. Mark my words."

"I've been marking them for some time now, Cailleach, and it looks like they're all still here. Where exactly has pushing me out of the picture got you? You know as well as I do that it's not our place to drive living creatures from their homes; it goes against our very nature. Humans won't be shifted so easily. We'll find ways to live in balance with them, I'm certain of that."

Cailleach's face didn't so much as flicker at Rosemary's words. Blair had the uneasy sense that in the guardian's eyes, very little had changed.

At last, Cailleach took a deep breath and drew herself together. "Then we part ways at last, Bodach."

"Couldn't come quickly enough, old friend," Rosemary said cheerfully. "And the name's Rosemary Duncan. Remember?"

She waggled her eyebrows at Blair and Alasdair and jerked her head for them to follow. They walked away together, leaving Cailleach standing on the shore. The kelpie-horse trotted after them, the brùnaidh gliding along in their wake.

It was full dark now, without the moon – but there were no clouds either, and the contours of the hills stood out in relief against the blue-black sky.

"I can't begin to thank you both for what you've done

for me today," Rosemary said as they walked back towards the steading.

Blair and Alasdair only looked at each other. Breaking the curse had been a happy accident really, the thing that had allowed Blair to save her home. There wasn't much credit to take.

"You needn't worry about old Cailleach any more." Rosemary seemed to sense the tension Blair couldn't quite shake. "She only has such power over you as you give to her."

Blair released her breath in a sigh. "I should never have accepted her bargain."

"Live and learn," said Rosemary cheerfully.

"But what did Cailleach mean when she said that you're 'human through and through' now?" Alasdair asked, wringing water from his T-shirt.

"Ah, that. Now that I've embraced humanity, no part of me is fey any more – including my lifespan. But between you and me, kids, immortality isn't all it's cracked up to be. Growing and ageing, changing, that's the flavour of life."

They climbed slowly to the ridge of the hills that overlooked the southern side of the island. Finally Blair saw the twinkling lights of the village ahead, and in the distance, a golden glow from the steading's windows, calling her home like a beacon.

"I know a shortcut to the village from here, Alasdair," Rosemary said. "And Blair – we'll see you tomorrow for the inspection."

Blair made a face. "Wish us luck."

Rosemary just chuckled. "You don't need it."

Blair hugged them both goodbye and then jogged away along the ridge towards her house. The kelpie-horse trotted beside her, breaking into a canter as they descended to the machair. Moss was an inky silhouette against the stars overhead.

Dancing golden will-o'-the-wisps guided them across the bog, and as they drew closer to the steading and the sea beyond it, Blair heard a resonant mooing from the shore. In the yellow light that spilled from the house she could see a herd of shaggy, seaweedy crodh mara grazing on the beach.

As she walked up to the back door, Blair noticed that a light was on in the sitting room. Through the window, she could see her parents curled up on a sofa together, both of them reading, their legs entwined.

The day of the inspection dawned bright and clear. There had been showers overnight, cooling the air and washing the island clean. Through her window, Blair saw her mum wading into the sea: she wasn't going to miss her morning swim, even on a day as important as this.

Blair was finally dry, following a hot shower and a deep sleep. The thought of stepping into that cold water after all she'd been through the previous night sent shivers down her spine: not today.

She got dressed and opened her bedroom door a crack. Her dad was reading at the kitchen table over a plate of toast, and he lifted his eyes over his book at the creaking of the door.

"Before you say anything, I'm sorry about last night," Blair said quickly.

Her dad finished crunching his mouthful of toast. "Pop the kettle on and we'll put it behind us."

Blair gave him a small smile as she stepped into the kitchen. She filled the kettle from the tap and flicked the switch.

"I'll make your herbata," she promised. "I'll be back by the time it's boiled."

Her dad chewed his toast and watched her go without further comment.

On bare feet, Blair skipped out into the garden, down the path and over the road. Her mum was already emerging from the water by the time Blair reached the shore, and they each stopped where they were, looking at the other. Why was it so much harder to speak now?

"I didn't mean what I said last night," Blair blurted at last.

"I'm your mother," Anna replied. "Don't you think I know when you're lying?"

Blair rushed forwards, closing the gap between them, and threw her arms around her mum. "I'm sorry," she said, tears pricking at her eyes. "I'm really sorry. About everything."

Her mum hesitated for a moment, perhaps too shocked to move, but then she enfolded Blair in her arms and squeezed her tight. "I know," she murmured against

Blair's hair. After a moment, she added: "You can make it up to us this morning."

The next few hours were spent dusting, straightening out bedding and hanging the final few picture frames on the walls. Before they knew it, the doorbell was ringing.

When Blair opened the front door, the committee came pouring in, greeting her genially: Mr Okafor from the general store, the ferryman with his yellow mackintosh, the old man from the Sea Stag Inn, and half a dozen more of Roscoe's senior residents. Morag rolled in, pushed by Rosemary, who winked at Blair as she passed. They were all wearing bright purple *ROSCOE NEEDS YOU!* badges.

Bringing up the rear were the Reids. Aileen's eyes shone as she looked around, drinking everything in. Her gaze landed on Blair, flicked quickly to her wrist – and, seeing nothing there, back to Blair's face. She smiled at her with genuine relief.

Alasdair walked in last, holding Ewan's hand.

"What a transformation!" Morag exclaimed.

"Wouldn't recognise the place, would you?" Mr Okafor agreed.

"Allow us to give you the grand tour," Blair's dad said with an affected bow, and the committee all tittered and followed him out to the hallway.

Blair hung back in the kitchen with Alasdair and Ewan. She went to the cupboards and began to unload bowls and cutlery.

Alasdair sidled up beside her. "Doesn't look like the house has fallen down."

"Not quite." Blair grinned. Alasdair smiled broadly, nudging her with his shoulder, then took the stack of bowls from her hands and began to set them at places around the table.

Blair started laying out the cutlery. "How did it go with your mum and dad?" she asked. "We never got to talk about it last night."

"Well, we were a bit preoccupied," Alasdair said. But he bobbed his head from side to side. "Could have been worse," he concluded. "The jury's still out on whether it was all a misunderstanding, or if Mum really knew what she was doing. But Dad says he misses home. He's thinking about dividing his time between land and sea. So we'll get to see him, either way."

"That's good." Blair smiled with relief. "You know I'm—"

"If you tell me you're sorry one more time," Alasdair warned, but there was a smirk on his lips. He turned to his younger brother, who was pulling books off a shelf and stacking them on the floor. "Hey, Ewan. I think you need a tour too!"

They showed Ewan the owl's nest in the rushes outside, then took him to greet the kelpie-horse grazing on the machair, and finally they all settled on Blair's bedroom floor with pastels and sketchbooks.

When the adults burst into the kitchen some time later, Blair and the boys abandoned their work in favour of food. The committee members were chattering amongst themselves so noisily Blair's dad could hardly make himself heard.

"Now we have a special treat for you," he announced to the group. "A traditional Polish recipe from my family: bigos, or hunter's stew, with fresh bread baked by my English wife."

The room was filled with chatter as they tucked into the meal, but before long Morag was raising her glass and tapping it with a spoon. The conversation around the table faded away.

"Can I have everybody's attention, please? Thank you. We all know why we're here today. Before the Zielinskis moved to Roscoe, the steading was pure and simply uninhabitable. Now – well, in short, the place is unrecognisable; but at the same time, you've preserved its true character, and its long history on this island.

"We've all witnessed how hard you've worked over such a short period of time to get the place ready for the festival. Since my tireless mother established it nigh on forty years ago, the Wild Roscoe Festival has brought a month of excitement and activity to our island on an annual basis. It's a grand old time for all of us to come together and share the magic of our wild island with the rest of the world. Now we're only a matter of days away from the start, and we couldn't be happier to have such a dedicated, charming young family running our newest business. It will come as no surprise to anyone here to announce that you've passed the inspection with flying colours."

Blair watched her parents' faces break into matching delighted smiles. And she was very surprised to find a wave of relief and happiness almost overwhelm her.

"There's one important thing missing, of course," Morag said loudly over the chatter that immediately bubbled up. "You still haven't told us the name of the place!"

Blair's parents beamed at each other, then looked at Blair.

"We thought we'd leave this one to our daughter," her dad said.

Blair felt the eyes of everyone at the table turn to her and her mouth went dry. "I've been working on it," she said, pushing her glasses up her nose. "What do you think about… the Fox & Owl?"

Aileen made a small sound, halfway between a sniffle and a sob. Blair's parents were smiling at each other again. Her mum took hold of Blair's hand and squeezed it.

"I think it's perfect," her dad said firmly.

"Roscoe Needs You will be proud to endorse the Fox & Owl Bed and Breakfast," Morag announced, with great ceremony. She raised her glass, and everyone around the table followed suit. "To the Zielinski family!"

THE LAST DAY
OF SUMMER

Everyone was gone; the house was finally quiet again. Blair's dad was washing the dishes by hand, apparently forgetting the newly installed dishwasher, while her mum dried. Blair ducked into her room and brought out her sketchbook. Her heart fluttered as she approached her parents.

"Mum, Tata," she began. "You know the big white wall of the outbuildings that faces the road?"

She had their attention now; both stopped what they were doing to look round at her. She flipped her sketchbook over so they could see her work. "I was thinking… It's a bit boring to look at, right? But if this was there instead… It might make it a bit more exciting for the guests when they arrive. I don't know…"

She trailed off. She'd been expecting her parents to interrupt much sooner, and this silence was unnerving.

Her mum and dad looked at each other and something passed between them that Blair couldn't name.

"It's beautiful, Blair," her dad said at last. "It'll be just the thing we need to stand out."

Blair's heart leapt into her throat. A smile burst onto her face. "I'll make a proper plan right now!" she said, and ran back into her room.

The following morning, Blair was up with the dawn. She selected the colours she'd need, filled a jar with white spirit, cracked open a tin of paint, grabbed a brush and got to work.

Over the course of the day, her parents came and went, watching but never commenting. Her mum went for her swim, and her dad sat in a deck chair to read his book from a good vantage point to spy on the owl's nest. And Blair worked, cleaning brushes and setting them out to dry, stirring up tins of paint and mixing colours. Bit by bit, she painted her first mural.

By mid-afternoon she was still in her pyjamas, now spotted with paint. There was a streak of black across her cheek, too, though she didn't know it. She dropped the brush she was holding and stepped back to admire her work.

Against a backdrop of hazy blue sky, a short-eared owl spread its wings wide in flight, caramel and burnt umber and cream, its violet eyes aglow either side of its black beak. Sitting on its haunches below, with the emerald and lavender hills beyond, a fluffy-coated red fox gazed up at the owl. Beneath the two animals, in cursive lettering, was written *The Fox & Owl Bed and Breakfast*.

Blair hadn't noticed her parents approach, but now her dad pulled her under one arm and her mum under the other and hugged them close. Both of her parents were smiling from ear to ear.

The owl who'd inspired the mural emerged suddenly over the top of the outbuildings, soaring over their heads as though she knew this was her moment.

"Her name's Moss, by the way," Blair told her parents.

Her dad blinked rapidly and then nodded. "Moss," he repeated, trying it out. "Moss. Yes, I suppose it suits her."

Moss glided back around to the roof and perched above their heads, looking right at Blair and hooting contentedly.

Blair set off into the hills a little while later, having finally changed from her pyjamas into a T-shirt and shorts. Bog cotton and heather scratched against her legs as she walked up the gentle slope, but not in an unpleasant way. In one hand she clutched the slimy riverweed bridle, its reins trailing in the long grass as she walked. She could hear the kelpie-horse's soft, reassuring hoofbeats as he followed her.

At the standing stone she stopped and turned back, and there was the view she had come to love, of the not-so-ramshackle house nestled between the machair and the sea. For a moment she just stood there, soaking it in.

The horse stopped too, looking at her curiously. She took a deep breath and walked up to him, sank her hands into the warm hair of his neck, and pressed her forehead against his.

When she held up the bridle, the whites of his eyes flashed and his nostrils flared in a snort. She braced herself for the transformation, then lifted the reins and threw them over his neck.

They missed. He had jumped backwards out of reach, and the reins landed anticlimactically in the grass. Blair furrowed her brow, gathered the reins up again and readied herself.

"I'm giving you your freedom!" she told him. She took a step closer and held out her hand. He nuzzled into it, his soft velvety lips brushing over her skin. She raised the bridle, but again he flinched. When she tried to put the reins over his head this time, he ran backwards, then turned and trotted away to a safe distance.

"Fine!" Blair shouted, then laughed. She looked down at the bridle in her hands – that strange, otherworldly object – and tossed it into the heather.

She walked up to the horse, offering her hands again, and when he was sure they were empty he allowed her to come close, resting his head on her shoulder.

"I guess we're stuck together now," said Blair. "But if you're going to hang around, we'll need something to call you."

The truth was, she'd been thinking about this for quite a while, and she kept finding herself returning to that moment when the kelpie had first appeared through the sea mist.

"How about Rouk?" she suggested gently.

The kelpie-horse dropped his head and snorted, and she took that as a yes.

When she turned back towards the house, Blair saw a familiar figure trudging up the slope towards them. It was Alasdair, his camera hanging from his neck, clad in hiking trousers and boots as usual. He had an envelope in his hand.

"Hey!" he called as he approached, waving his free hand over his head. "I just went to the house looking for you. Your mum asked me to bring you this. It just arrived."

Blair took the letter. The scribble of her name and address on the front was familiar, but for a moment she couldn't place it. Then she ripped the envelope open and a spectrum of colour flooded out. It was a teenage girl's scrawl, bordered with vibrant patterns and illustrations.

My dear Blair,

You're right. Since modern communications are CLEARLY not working for us, the old-fashioned way will have to do! Now, let me tell you everything you've missed in my life, and then I have some questions for you...

Blair's heart surged as she scanned the letter's contents, and her eyes landed on the bottom of the fifth page.

Your unbelievably patient and ever-loyal,
Libby
xoxo

Blair held the letter to her chest and blinked back the tears that were threatening to fall.

"Friend from your old school?" he asked.

Blair nodded. She wasn't quite ready to speak.

"We go back next week," Alasdair said. At Blair's grimace, he went on: "I was thinking about the protest you were telling me about. When we, um, first met." He had the good grace to look a little embarrassed. "We have to get the ferry to the nearest island to go to school. I was thinking that it might be cool if we, um… missed the ferry."

Blair felt a smile creeping unstoppably across her face. "You want to strike!"

Alasdair shrugged sheepishly. "I just want you to know… It's not like I didn't understand. I just didn't want to hear it. But I started looking up what you guys have been doing in Carlisle. It's like Rosemary said – we have to find ways to live in balance. Which is exactly what you're all trying to tell people."

Blair felt tears prickling in her eyes again; she bit her bottom lip to hold them back.

"I know kids from the other islands," Alasdair was saying. "I thought maybe we should start messaging them. I'm sure we could get a lot of other students to strike with us. We could take photos with signs on all the different islands, or something. It'd probably be one of the most remote school strikes in the world, right? Might be good for—"

He was cut off when Blair threw her arms around him and lifted him clear off the ground.

"Have I ever told you you're my favourite person?"

He wriggled free of her embrace, but his cheeks were pink. "Give me some warning next time you're planning to go airborne!"

Blair clapped her hands together, the letter between her palms. "Oh Alasdair, you have no idea what you've started. With the festival happening at the same time – all those people coming from far and wide to see the amazing wildlife on *our* island…"

Alasdair grinned. "No better time to make our voices heard."

On the morning of the last day of summer, Blair laced up her boots and headed out the door. Today, she was determined, she would finally walk the entire coast of her small island. Without a word from Blair, Rouk cantered over from the far side of the machair and fell in behind her, his head bobbing as his hooves ate up the ground.

It was a beautiful day for it: light cloud streaking across the blue sky in the breeze, the sun warm on Blair's arms. She was wearing sunscreen today, with a waterproof packed in her rucksack just in case, alongside a full water bottle, snacks, and her sketchbook. She felt like a different person to the city girl who had set out in search of a kelpie all those weeks ago.

She and Rouk took the path around the outskirts of the village, which was a hive of activity. People were hanging bunting between lampposts, setting up stalls around the harbour, turning a field into a temporary campsite, putting signs in windows and hanging banners from boats on the water.

When Blair crossed the bridge over the river she waved at Irving, who was drifting on their back, letting the current carry them downstream as they played with their otter friend.

By late morning Blair and Rouk had reached Whalebone Bay. Blair ran her hand over the bleached bones, but this time nothing stirred. Seal and human heads bobbed in the surf beyond, and far out in the ocean, the curve of a black back and a tall fin cut through the waves.

Beyond the bay, Blair followed the path along the north coast to the sea loch. The ground was still furrowed where it had been carved up by the Fiadh Mho'r's hooves. Will-o'-the-wisps glittered on the path that would lead her through the hills, back to the steading.

There was so much joy in the air. She may be starting over at a new school, but she had Alasdair, and she knew she could survive it. She was a Zielinski, after all. She didn't need to be at the centre of things; she was going to change the world from a tiny island in the Atlantic Ocean. And she was lucky – so unbelievably lucky – to get to live somewhere wild and beautiful that reminded her what she was fighting for every single day.

Her parents had given her that.

It was early evening by the time she reached the standing stone at the top of the hill above the steading. She could see the village in the distance, and the white shape of a ferry pulling into the harbour. A tide of people disembarked on foot. They were the first tourists of the season, she realised. Her quiet home was about to become a lot busier.

In the hills, a stag roared. It echoed, and a moment later it was joined by another voice, and another. Blair looked up into the heights of the Creachanns, and she thought she saw a tall, commanding woman with a crown of antlers on the highest ridge. The figure walked in the midst of a herd of deer, but they passed out of sight behind a rocky outcrop. All that emerged on the far side was the herd, led by a stag with many-pronged antlers.

Rouk snorted at Blair's shoulder and she turned to rest her head against his neck. She could see the inviting shape of the steading on the edge of the silver sea, the distant speck of an owl wheeling in circles above it. She whistled to Rouk and together they ran across the machair towards home.

THE END

GLOSSARY

bean nighe: (pronounced 'ben nee-yeh') in Scottish folklore, a washerwoman who foretells of danger

bigos: (pronounced 'bee-ghos') a traditional Polish stew with sauerkraut and sausage, sometimes called 'hunter's stew' in English

bodach: (pronounced 'bot-ackh') in Scottish folklore, a trickster, but also the name for an old man

bog: wet, spongy ground, usually too soft to walk upon without sinking

brùnaidhs: (pronounced 'brownies' or 'broonies') spirits of the home

burn: Scots word for 'stream'

Cailleach: (pronounced 'kal-yuch') in Celtic folklore, an ancient goddess

Cat-sìth: (pronounced 'cat-shee') in Celtic folklore, a fairy cat

crodh mara: (pronounced 'cro mara') in Scottish folklore, fairy cattle

Cù-sìth: (pronounced 'coo-shee') in Celtic folklore, a phantom hound

fey: anything relating to the magical world; fey folk = fairy folk

Fiadh Mho'r: (pronounced 'fee-ugh vore'), a monstrous sea-stag

herbata: a Polish tea, often served with sugar and lemon

heteronormative: the assumption that everyone is heterosexual (straight) and cisgender (identifying with the gender you were assigned at birth) and that this is the default way of being

kelpie: in Scottish folklore, a shapeshifting water creature

kochanie: (pronounced 'ko-han-ya') Polish term of affection, similar to 'darling' or 'honey'

machair: (pronounced 'mackh-ur') coastal, marshy grasslands with lots of wildflowers – a rare habitat found only in north-west Scotland and Ireland

moor: an open area of often marshy land, covered with rough grass

myszka: (pronounced 'miz-kah') Polish for 'little mouse'

non-binary: people who do not identify as male or female, but as neither, or a mixture of genders, and may use gender-neutral pronouns such as 'they' instead of 'he' or 'she'

orca: a toothed whale in the dolphin family, sometimes known as a 'killer whale'

peat: soil found in boggy areas, sometimes burned as fuel

phosphorescence: a faint light that is emitted without any noticeable heat

redcap: in Scottish folklore, a kind of goblin that often lives in castle ruins

rouk: (pronounced 'rook') a Scots word for mist that drifts in from the sea

sauerkraut: (pronounced 's-ow-er-krowt') fermented cabbage

sea loch: similar in appearance to a lake, but actually part of the sea, mostly surrounded by land

selkies: in Celtic folklore, seals who can take human form

sluagh: (pronounced 'sloo-ugh') in Celtic mythology, flying souls of the restless dead

Tata: Polish word for 'Dad'

transgender: identifying with a different gender from the one you were assigned at birth. Transgender people often change their appearance, name and pronouns (e.g. from 'she' to 'he') so that they feel more like themselves. This term can include non-binary people.

uplands: a hilly area, similar to highlands

will-o'-the-wisps: in folklore, ghostly guiding lights

Wulver: in Scottish mythology, a kind of werewolf

ABOUT THE AUTHOR

Alex Mullarky (they/them) is a writer, veterinary nurse and the author of *The Sky Beneath the Stone*. They transport injured seals as a Marine Mammal Medic and scan the sea for whales and dolphins with Shorewatch. Their work with wildlife inspires their stories about nature and magic.

Alex lives on the edge of Edinburgh with their family and loves to explore Scotland's wild coasts and islands in their free time. They can often be found wild swimming, playing roller derby, or running along the beach with their dog Finn.

AUTHOR'S NOTE

Facing the climate crisis can feel overwhelming. If you are experiencing eco-anxiety as a reader, please visit my website (alexmullarky.com) for some links and resources that you may find helpful.

If you're a young person with questions about your gender identity, Mermaids can offer advice and support. Visit mermaidsuk.org.uk to speak to someone.

ACKNOWLEDGEMENTS

Thank you to my agent Zoë Plant for finding the true name of the B&B (among many other things) and to Martha for your support. To the whole team at Floris Books, especially my editor Jennie Skinner, for being a joy to work with and for bringing this book to life. To Ramune Kregzdyte for perfectly capturing the wild magic of Roscoe in your gorgeous cover art.

Thank you to Katharine Philp, Meegan May, Tori Larsen, Lucy Hayes and Kelly Case for your invaluable feedback over the years. To Marta Grosicka, consultant on all things Polish and an excellent next-door neighbour. To Tadek, Łukasz and Iwona for your insights on early drafts. To Jennie, Dave and Hugh for lending me your surname.

At the Scottish Owl Centre, to Trystan, Nicole, and most importantly Mac (the short-eared owl) for sharing your expertise. To research buddy and photographer Mairhi Macleod. To Tine Van de Velde for your beautiful interpretations of Blair and Cailleach.

I was lucky enough to work on this book during a retreat at Moniack Mhor, and to spend a week sailing around the Small Isles with Sail Britain gathering inspiration.

Thank you to my fellow participants on both trips for your encouragement, and special thanks to Catherine and Jenny for leading a wonderful voyage on board *Merlin*.

'The Lynx and the Plague' is adapted from the Polish folktale 'The Plague and the Peasant', collected by John T. Naaké. It's no secret that much of my source material is the folklore of Scotland, a country I have now called home as long as I have anywhere else. I don't think I could ever tire of hearing, reading and retelling these tales, nor should we.

Publishing a book can be tough, so thank you to all the authors, booksellers, teachers, librarians and festival teams who have been so friendly and welcoming. Special thank you to the Andersons and to Skye McKenna for your guidance and friendship.

I was very fortunate to receive an Authors Foundation grant from the Society of Authors to work on this book. Thank you SoA, for this and also for your events and advocacy.

Thank you to everyone who read, reviewed and told their friends about *The Sky Beneath the Stone*, and thank YOU for reading this story, which is so close to my heart.

Finally, thank you to my family of frogs: Laurel, Jill and Finn.